An Uncomfortable Conversation

By Derrick Anthony Marrow

Warning and Disclaimer: This is going to be a very tough read for some. What you will see in the following pages is the truthful interaction between two men. The publishing of this conversation is meant as the start of the conversation. Hopefully a conversation you will find yourself joining into as you read through the pages. It is meant as both a conversation for self-reflection and reflection on the outlook you have for others. Hopefully you will take a look at your values, your truths and the respect we all should share. Some of the words, the ideas presented in this dialogue you will agree with and some you will vehemently disagree with. These are the words of two men who decided they needed to sit down, look each other square in the eye and have an open and honest conversation. It might not have been easy but to have a real conversation each participant had to listen to the other person. Not listen to react and counter argue but listen to understand. Hopefully as you read you will find yourself sitting at the table with these two people. Thank you for adding to the discussion. Here we go.

1| Opening Lines of Communication   pg. 1

2| What They Came Here For   pg. 33

3| As They Continue Conversating   pg. 62

4| Learning is Hard Work   pg. 77

5| Growth Takes Time   pg. 93

6| Opening Minds   pg. 102

7| Ends Are New Beginnings   pg. 123

1| Opening Lines of Communication

"How did we get here?"

"We got here because you offered to fight me. As if I was going to take some threat from some random person online serious."

"And that right there is the problem. No I didn't offer to fight you. I offered you an invitation to talk. What I said to you was and I quote 'Enough of this back and forth over social media if you really want to talk we can do it in person.' Now you took that as a threat and an offer to a fight but physical violence was never intended. I think you're initial response was sad but I can't control how you perceive words that I never said and I never mentioned anything about fighting. My question to you though is why? What would make you think I would want to put my hands on you for something you said to me especially over the internet? I'm a grown man with kids and bills. I'm not some internet troll. You could clearly see my picture. That's my face in my avatar and me putting my hands on you won't do anything to make anything better. It wouldn't even make me feel better beating you up over something you said online. Who does that? But back to my original question. Why did you think those words were an invitation to fight when no such words were uttered or rather typed?"

"I read between the lines. Your reply to my statement was gruff and abrupt. It cut off the dialogue we were having. To me the nature of the way the conversation went, I thought you were insinuating you wanted to fight? And how was I supposed to know the picture was really you. Do you know how many fake accounts there are out there in cyber space? Safety is always my primary concern. I've been in enough situations where exactly what you said turned violent. When someone says let's step outside there's no mention of violence in the actual words spoken but you know what's going to happen when you get out there."

"But there was no outside to go. We were in completely different places, different cities in different states. So you read between the lines. Are you sure you want to do this now. Are you sure you're safe. Safety concerns aren't a concern right now? You don't think I'm going to just go off and punch you now do you?"

"No. Let's just say I vetted you before I came here."

"As you should. As I did you. So we're here to have an honest conversation right? To pick up where we left off which was nowhere really."

"Yes. I think we both have some things we need to say and maybe a few things we need to hear."

"You know this is going to get heated at some points? Are you really ready to hear what most people don't want to? What most people are afraid to hear?"

"I'm fully aware of what lies ahead today. If you're one hundred percent honest with me I'll be one hundred percent honest with you."

"I plan on being one hundred percent truthful. If not this meeting will get us nowhere and you would have come all this way for nothing."

"As do I."

"I will not pull any punches."

"I got it. You wanted to talk, man to man, face to face, let's do it."

"Good. Well let's start with the truth right now. If I wasn't a black male. And I'm not even a very imposing one. I'm not six two, two hundred and fifty pounds. I'm not built like a linebacker and I don't cut much of an imposing figure by size. Maybe by aura but not by sheer size. But you couldn't see that online. So if I wasn't a black man, or maybe portraying a black man since you weren't sure if I was really me online, if I wasn't a black man would you have thought I was asking you to a fight. If I was a woman, an Asian man or maybe another white man as yourself. Would you have thought the same?"

"Truthfully? If you were a woman. No. If you were an Asian man, no. Unless your online profile said you were in the Triad or something, then maybe but realistically no. Now this is going to surprise you a little. If you were a white man, maybe, probably. Unless you were an academic, a professor somewhere I would have thought the same thing."

"I know what an academic is but I'm glad you said that. Why? Why out of all the people in the world you would have read into the posts of a white man, maybe, but definitely a black man in a violent nature? Is that the way you see people? Do you usually stereotype people based on their skin color?"

"It's the way I see people online. Everybody's a tough guy on line. Especially when you don't agree with them. The anonymity gives people courage to say things they wouldn't say to your face. But that's why we're here right. To look into each other's eyes and say it to their face?"

"To a certain extent yes. But more importantly, hopefully, we're here to learn. I'm here to see things through the prism of your eyes, your upbringing, your history. So let me ask you this. The way you see people online, is that the way you see them in real life?"

"To a certain extent yes. Minus the tough guy part but yeah I'd say so."

"Do you even see what you're doing?"

"What do you mean?"

"I mean a minute ago you gave a nuanced answer to how you see people. You didn't lump everyone together into one category. You broke it down into, I see my interactions with these people as this but these people as something different. You simply stated yes you stereotyped me and all black people and all non-academic white people. I'm, sorry all black males and all non-academic white males."

"Whether justifiable or not we all fall back on stereotypes. Can you sit here and tell me you don't?"

"I can."

"You're lying."

"You don't even know me nor have you heard what I have to say yet and you're already calling me a liar. A rational person would at least wait until they knew I lied before assuming I did."

"Everyone has stereotypes. You don't have to admit it to yourself but everyone does. It's an inherent part of life."

"It's not a part of life because they are not a part of nature. Stereotypes are learned behavior taught by other people. So not me. I don't have any stereotypes. I don't live my life that way. And before you continue on with your argument let me explain why. First I will agree with your point to a certain extent. Yes, most people fall back on the stereotypes they've learned over the years. But this is why I don't. It limits one's self to look at others and think you know something about them because of a false set of data which is what stereotypes are."

"Stereotypes are not false data. They all come from a basis in reality."

"From a false reality. Listen, if I look at every white person or brown person or every female or every whatever category or person I'm referencing then I don't look at you for you. Who you really are. I'm never going to give you a chance to be whatever you are because my vision is blurred. That's what stereotypes to, they blind you to the truth because you hung up on some narrative. Now once you prove who you are either positive or negative then that's another story. See that's the problem with stereotypes. They are a narrative which ultimately almost never fits the individual person."

"So you're admitting some people fit the stereotype about their group."

"How many people how you known that fit the stereotype you thought. I'm talking about people you know, not what's flashed on a tv screen because you never know the truth or the intricacies of what's going on there."

"None to be truthful. But that's because I would never let anyone like that in my circle."

"Anyone like what? See you're doing it now. You're assuming I'm talking about stereotypical black people. But there are stereotypes for every race, creed, religion, etcetera etcetera."

"So you're telling me you take everybody for who they are, you never had any preconceived notions, not a slight thought of who someone was just by looking at them. By the way they dress or the way they're acting?"

"I'm telling you it took me a long time to get there. It took me many missed opportunities and many mistakes to get there."

"Opportunities?"

"Not opportunities like this person may have some kind of financial windfall for me or could get me a better paying job. I meant opportunities to learn, to grow, to expand one's horizons. Women who would have been beautiful mates, a great girlfriend, maybe even a great wife. Not that I'm mad because I love my wife. She is a Godsend. And there are other examples. Stereotypes are nothing more than racism."

"Whoa, whoa. Now you're taking it too far."

"No I'm not. Take out your phone and google racism. What does it say?"

"Alright, let me look. Ok, it says racism is the belief in the superiority of one race over another, which often results in discrimination and prejudice towards people based on their race or ethnicity."

"Now google stereotype."

"It says, stereotype is any thought widely adopted about specific types of individuals or certain ways of behaving intended to represent the entire group of those individuals or behaviors as a whole. These thoughts or beliefs may or may not accurately reflect reality."

"So both racism and stereotypes deal with a person, a single person looking at another different group of people and believing they know something about them. Racists believe they are superior to every other group and most stereotypes, the damaging ones are where someone believes in something negative about another group enhancing their belief of superiority. Both are learned behaviors past down from other people."

"I see where you are going but every stereotype isn't racist."

"It may not always be a one-to-one comparison but more often than not they are. That lady on whatever tv show that was didn't say I'm going to Jew you down as a positive comment about Jewish people and their finances."

"She said that on tv and they let it get part their censors?"

"Yes sir but even that illustrates my point. The people who were doing the checking didn't even realize it was offensive. At the minimum both ideals, stereotyping and racism are lazy. And at the maximum both ideas are dangerous. Both stop someone, a single person from dealing with another group of people. And whether you want to admit it or not this country has a problem with both."

"But not all people are either."

"You're right. There is no such thing as every when it comes to people and that's not what I'm saying anyway."

"C'mon man. Most stereotypes are based on the truth where racism, especially this definition is not."

"Not true. Most stereotypes are based on the amalgamation, you like that word don't you, most stereotypes are based on the amalgamation of chosen aspects of different people bled together to form the narrative of the author. In other words most stereotypes are not true because they infer something from a small minority of people within a group and portray that thing to be the whole group. Normally the stereotype only fits an infinitesimal number within a group of people and even then it's patched together from different people to describe a person who never really truly existed. For every stereotype you name, if you were to get a group of people the stereotype supposedly depicts the overwhelming majority of the people it wouldn't fit. You'd be hard pressed to find even one. And even if you did the overwhelming majority would be pissed you described them as this false stereotype because it doesn't fit who they are."

"I could find you some that fit the description in every group."

"That's my point exactly though. You could find me one, maybe. And for everyone you find I could find you nine hundred and ninety nine thousand that it didn't fit. For example, you're a white man, are all white people racist?"

"No, but there are some that are."

"How many. What do you think the ratio is of white racist people to white non-racist people?"

"That's like asking how many ghetto black people are there?"

"See now you're getting offended. But what I'm not going to do is what a lot of black people have had to do all their lives and that is make you feel comfortable. I'm not here for that and hopefully neither are you. I'm not here to walk on the other side of the street because Becky doesn't feel comfortable when she sees me walking down a street. How do I know she's scared, because she starts gripping her pocketbook tight. She didn't grab her pocketbook when you walked by her but me I'm a black man so she's scared. You can lock your car doors when I drive by like I'm going to jump out and grab you. I'm not here to make you feel comfortable."

"Nobody asked you to make me feel comfortable. So just because I said the word ghetto when referring to black people, that word touched a nerve. So what if I said?"

"Said what, if you said what? Go ahead say it. I know what you want to say. I give you permission go ahead say it."

"Nah, I'm good and believe me when I say I don't need you permission."

"Then why don't you say it. What are you afraid of?"

"I'm not afraid of nothing in this room especially no word."

"That's good I don't want you to be afraid of anything in this room especially me. You're going to respect me but I don't want you to fear me

I'm just here to talk. But it always goes back to you thinking this black man, me, I have some penchant for violence doesn't it?"

Chuckles

"Nah don't laugh. Say the word. I want you to say it."

"I won't say the word. It's disrespectful. That's definitely not what we are here for right? But why is it ok for you to say the word and not for me?"

"Do you have a wife or girlfriend, sisters, mom, aunts, any kind of females you are close to?"

"Yes. What do they have to do with this?"

"Ever call one of them a bitch?"

"No. But hip-hop music does it all the time. Just like they say the n-word you want me to say. What makes it ok for them and you to say it and not me? Why can black people say it and not white people? That's not fair."

"Two things. First I like how you didn't say your hip-hop music. So you listen to rap. Cool. I like that. And I didn't say it was ok. But let's come back to the music in a minute. Let's go back to what you asked. Why is it ok for me to say the word nigga and not you? First some black people will tell you it's never ok. And I have to respect their opinion. I haven't lived the lives they've lived or dealt with some of the things they had to endure. The police have never turned hoses on me or set dogs loose on me so I have to respect that generation and why they are so against the word. I'm truly climbing a ladder they laid against the wall when they were arrested, beaten and killed for doing what, wanting to be equal? But the reason you can't say it is the same reason you can't call your wife, girlfriend, mother, coworker, aunt, or any woman a bitch. Women, and if you're around enough of them you'll hear them call each other bitches all the time. Maybe not all the time but enough. They use it as a term of

9 | P a g e

endearment when they're talking to themselves amongst themselves. They take no offense to it when it comes from their girlfriends. But you better not dare say that word to any woman. It's what happens with words. Words have power. So what happens is words with negative feelings, connotations associated with them, the words get repurposed by the group they are supposed to offend. If you were to call the women in your life bitches you might die and rightfully so. Even those rappers who use it in their songs don't call the women in their lives bitches or they might die. When words are repurposed by a group, and the power is removed from the word it becomes a word only usable by members of that group. That's the rule. No lie I heard a gay man call another gay man a faggot a few days ago. He said come on faggot let go its right up the street or something like that. And yes they were both gay, they weren't' hiding it. But I can't call a gay man that. That's why you can't use the n-word. That word, even though a lot of people don't like it, it is used with love amongst the group of people it was used as a slur against if that makes any sense to you. And if you were to say it, which I suggest you don't unless you want to die, the love wouldn't come across. That's also why it's a word used between friends except maybe for rappers and comedians. Black comedians."

"Then why don't white guys have a word like that."

"Because words like that have always come from the majority looking to intimidate a smaller group. White people to black people. Men to women. Straight people to gay people. Etcetera. Etcetera. It's also one of the reasons white males are afraid to be the minority."

"You talk in a lot of absolutes."

"I try not to because there are few to no absolutes in this world, everything has shades of grey. I just try to speak the truth. Some things I can answer and some things I can't. Some things I have opinions on, which I mostly keep to myself and others I don't."

"Well you have a lot of opinions about me and white people in general I see."

"I have no opinion of you because I don't know you. By the end of this conversation I will start to formulate one though. Tell me has there been anything I've said which isn't true? You ask I answer. Isn't that what we are here for? And it's because I don't have opinions I have facts. Not all white people are racist. Not all police are bad but it was white police who turned water hoses on black people. It was white racist people who burned down black churches. I'm just stating fact. I'm not putting that fact on all white people because there were white abolitionists, there were white people marching for equality, there are white people marching for equality today. That's crazy. Why in this day and time are people still marching for equality? Wow! Now, I'm not saying you did any of those things but just because you're not comfortable with the facts don't dismiss them like they didn't happen. But like I said, isn't that what we're here for?"

"It is."

"So how about this, I'll ask you in the form of a question. Why are white people afraid to be the minority?"

"Now who's stereotyping? Though I thought you were going to ask about the President."

"Oh I will. We'll get to that later. I'll put it in my notes, topics to come back to. Hip-Hop music and The President of the United States. But if I'm stereotyping, which you're right I am because I'm generalizing because I want you to answer, why are white people so scared to be the minority in America?"

"You know we don't have meetings. Every white man is not a member of the klan or the illuminati. We don't meet every Sunday in the Church's basement and plot to take over the world. We're all not Hitler."

Shrug. "So you're saying white people aren't afraid to become the minority in this country?"

"No. That's not what I'm saying. What I'm saying is the majority of white people don't discuss or even think about the topic. Most white people have too many other things to worry about. They go to work then come home and have to take care of their families and live their lives. Most white people are not concerned with becoming the minority group of people in the country. They could care less. The only ones who are, and yes I'm stereotyping since we seem to like doing that, the only ones that worry about an entire race becoming the minority are ones who are racists. Yes, I said it. Happy now?"

"Is what you just said the truth or are you trying to patronize me?"

"No. It's the truth."

"Then I'm happy. I can't be mad at the truth. I can not like it but I can't be mad it."

"The truth is most white people who worry about white people becoming the minority are racist. They might not admit it but they are. I grew up around them I know. They don't want to live next to black people. And they really don't want to live next to a Black Muslim. It is what it is. It shouldn't be that way but it is. But most of those people have never met a black person. They've never sat down with them. Some because of circumstance but most because of old fashioned stubbornness. And the ones that do then they rationalize it if they met a black person and realize they are a good person. They'll tell you they are the exception. Most of those people are just regurgitating rhetoric, now you like that word too don't you."

Laughs

"Yeah, most of those people are regurgitating rhetoric that's been taught to them. They don't know any better. It's like an engrained doctrine. Now there are exceptions like every now and then you get that one privileged little girl who thinks she deserves a spot at Harvard and when she doesn't get it wants to sue, she's not being racist she's just being spoiled but it comes across as racist. But this is a society who is ruled by lawsuit now. And I can see the look on your face. Yes I said it and I'll go even further. Most white people who worry about white people becoming the minority are racists or neo-nazi scumbags. Racists with no sense of history. Yes as a white man from the south I detest people like that. Yes there are people from the south who don't like the racist leanings of their neighbors. And before you ask yes, the 'alt-right' is just a coded word, a way of not trying to call them what they are which are racists. Listen to me. The overwhelming majority of white people are good hard working, love thy neighbor once they get to know them kind of people. We are not what we are portrayed to be. We are not white trash. We are not disposable."

"I'm curious then. What are black people portrayed to be. In your opinion."

"I don't think any group of people, American people are portrayed in the best light. Foreigners are portrayed to be great unless they're black or Muslim. Asian people are geniuses. We need them to come in and run anything that has to do with a computer. That HB, I forgot the number, but the HB Visa program for companies to bring individuals from outside the country to work. So called high-skilled individuals. That's nonsense. It's a way to bring in cheaper labor. Expensive in comparison to other jobs but cheaper than paying their American counterparts what they deserve. But nobody talks about them for whatever reason. And we're talking about companies who are making millions if not billions cutting American jobs to save a few hundred thousand. Also Europeans are seen as business masters. They're sexy and attractive. Now people from African countries and South American countries, they're all portrayed as third-world countries. I couldn't sit here and tell you of one country, even those with tourist destinations, in Africa or South America that gets shown in a positive light. Just like Americans. No group of Americans seem to be shown in a good light. We seem to publicize the worst of the worst here. Like why did you pick that person to put on tv. That is not a representation of me or my neighborhood or my city."

"Don't avoid the question. In your opinion how are black people portrayed?"

"Black people are not portrayed in the best light but like I said no one is. Black people are portrayed as gang bangers, drug dealers, or entertainers. You're never portrayed as intelligent. And the ones that are, are portrayed as outliers, exceptions. But white people are portrayed as racists and unintelligent backwater marry your sister toothless idiots so it's not just black people they make look like that. But that's not the way I look at people, not black people or white people or any people."

"How do you look at black people then?"

Deep breath. "I put all people in two categories. The people I know and the people I don't. I'm wary of all the people I don't know. The people I do know I put them in their proper context, category, place, whatever you want to call it."

"So when you see a black kid versus when you see a white kid, same age, same sex, you don't look at them any different."

"Man they're all kids."

"Ok. When you see a group of 10 white kids at the mall, what do you think about them compared to when you see a group of ten black kids at the mall?"

"I don't go to the mall."

"Ok, walking down the street, at the gas station, at the movie theater, whatever. You know what I'm asking."

"You're asking do I look at the two groups differently. If I fear the black kids more than I fear the white kids?"

"You used the word fear. I just asked what do you think when you see the two groups. You said white people are portrayed as this and black people are portrayed as this, both unfairly but when you see two group of kids you immediately have a reaction of fear, your word, towards the black kids. Why if you don't know either group? Why would a group of black kids scare you?"

"You're putting words in my mouth."

"You said it not me."

"I asked a question. I didn't make a statement. It's not fear so much as being cautious. It's the fear of the unknown. Not that I think I'm unsafe around them I'd just watch them a second longer then I would the white kids. I'm just being honest here. And as I say it out loud I know it's not right but it's the truth. It's what we see all over the television. Black kids running amuck. I know they don't show anything positive on tv but most crimes seem to be committed by black people so I'm a little more cautious around large groups of them especially younger kids who haven't grown and matured. It might not be right and I hate even saying now that I'm realizing what I'm saying it but I have a family that needs me and I want to go home at night. So if I have to be a little stereotypical in that view it is what it is. I want and need to be safe so if that includes stereotyping some kids I don't know so be it."

"Even if your fear, trepidation I'll call it is unwarranted."

"Better safe than sorry."

"Isn't that how Trayvon Martin was killed. Fear and trepidation from some wannabe cop with a gun."

Shakes his head. "Man I'm not him. Please don't even lump me in the same category with that guy. He wasn't even a white guy but I get the point."

"My point is the fear you have and many others share, though you believe yourself not to be racist"

"I am not but go ahead."

"The fear you have is the same fear that led to Trayvon Martin being killed. An unwarranted fear. A fear placed on a kid by a false narrative of black kids. By an unequal portrayal of black kids."

"But wasn't it because there were break-ins in that neighborhood by black kids."

"Not that one. So because some black kid did something every black kid is a suspect. The double standard is the problem. White kids commit crimes too and if a white kid had been breaking into homes every white kid walking down the street wouldn't have been suspicious. The fear out there is ridiculous. And this fear has you somewhat blinded to the truths, it's ridiculous."

"What truths?"

"That the portrayal of black people is unequal. The narrative is false."

"Why do you say it's an unequal portrayal?"

"Because they pick and choose who they want to show and how they want to show them. For every black kid they show doing something illegal there's a white kid in the same area doing the same thing. But it doesn't fit the narrative so they don't show it. Even where you grew up I'm positive they probably showed you the black man two towns over doing crime and not the white guy living on your block. When a black man commits a crime his face gets plastered all over tv immediately. When it's a white man they always have to wait. Where you lived think about who did the crimes in real life versus who was shown on tv being arrested. This false portrayal leads to fear, your fear. The fear that cost a kid, numerous black kids their lives."

"First it can't be a false portrayal if they really did it. It might not be equal but it isn't false. There is a very distinct difference there your skipping over. Now fear, my fear, your fear, everyone's fear is one's way of making sure one's self is safe. Fear is never unwarranted as you suggested. It may be misapplied but it is never unwarranted. Fear keeps you from touching the fire. Fear keep you alive. Now I wasn't there when it happened. That kid, it's unfortunate what"

"Can you say his name?"

"I can. Trayvon Martin. His name is Trayvon Martin and he should be alive today. It's unfortunate what happened to him it really is. That kid did not deserve to die. I can't say it no other way."

"You're stating the obvious. He was unarmed."

"No I'm not stating the obvious. A kid lost his life and we as a country debated why he was there like walking down the street is a crime. It wasn't and the spectacle that became of it was unbecoming of the country I went to war for. Where my brother lost lives. This kid did nothing wrong and lost his life for no other reason than because he was black. It really is that simple. We as a country need to stop finding excuses for wrong. You don't have to say to me what has been said before. If that was a black man who killed a white child we would be having a different conversation. This I know. What I'm also doing is making a statement for all the white people out there who have to answer this question like we are somehow the representatives of the whole white race. We didn't pull the trigger. We didn't kill Trayvon Martin. That kid did not deserve to die. His mother should have never had to shed those tears. But I, we had nothing to do with his death and I'm tired of speaking about it like I have to defend myself."

"You shouldn't. But I'm also tired of having to explain to my child the realities of living in America while black and no matter what you say these are not false realities. This place is no utopia. Don't get me wrong it's the best, by far and bar none, it's the best place to live on the planet but it's far from perfect. And until I die I'm allowed to address the imperfections. But when we do people get upset. This President can say let's make America great again like it wasn't already, but when people address social issues it's, no don't do that, it's better than everywhere else. See the conflict there? So let me ask where do you think this fear of young black men comes from?"

"I'll tell you exactly where it comes from. Where I grew up, there wasn't a ton of black families. Maybe one on the other side of town. So growing up the only frame of reference I had about black people was from tv. TV including the news and television shows and music. I'll start first with the news. I can't remember one news clip of something positive a black person did. I'm sure there were some but because of the deluge of negative stories the positive ones were easily forgotten. Two tv shows. Outside of the Cosby show which I never watched or even heard of until I got older, what positive light was shown about black people on television, if they were even on the show? If they were they were butlers. Then there is the music. I love rap music. I listened to it my whole life. But it wasn't the most positive when it comes to the image of black people. Everybody was bitches and gangsters and drug dealers."

"Wait, you're going to blame, at least lay part of the blame of your negative stereotypes of black people on the music. Do you blame the violence and murders on movies? Is Arnold Schwarzenegger responsible for war and violence or Al Pacino for drugs, you know he is Scarface and they play that movie thousands a time a year?"

"No that's ridiculous. But I didn't listen to movies two hundred times over and over and over again. Movies don't have the same beat. And movies are fake. Those stories in rap music are real."

"First every story in rap music isn't real. And what about all the positive music. The BDP's, the Self-Destruction's, the PE's of the world."

"Outside of Public Enemy if that's who you mean by PE I never listened to any of that."

"So what you listened to did you understand what they were saying. When NWA said Fuck the Police did you understand why? When Nas or Big or Jay or Pac said whatever they said did you understand the message?"

"I wasn't listening to the music for a message. I just liked the music. When NWA said Fuck the Police I said Fuck the Police. I didn't understand why they were saying what they were saying I just liked the song."

"So first you didn't understand what you were listening to. Second you didn't care to listen to if for what it was. Third you only got out of it what you wanted to hear anyway. So you took an entire culture, please understand hip-hop is a culture, and obviously a culture you have no clue about and you simplified it down to a beat. You took a song about police brutality and ignored the message behind the hook. A hook designed to draw you in to their story of police brutality."

"If you want to say it like that then yes. I couldn't relate to the stories they were telling. That wasn't my reality. I couldn't fathom half the stuff they were saying. So to me it was like a movie, not real. I mean I took their stories as their truth but it wasn't real to me. Plus as a kid can you really understand the depth of songs?"

"Someone once said if you give them control of the music it doesn't matter who makes the laws. Music is the voice of the youth and you didn't pay attention. And you're not alone there. So you didn't believe what was in the not real movie but you believed what was in the not real music as real. Then you took all the negative aspects of the music, ignored all the positive aspects of the culture the music was representing and you let those feed your stereotypes of us. That's some of the laziest most hypocritical nonsense I've ever heard."

"I never looked at it like that. I wasn't trying to be hypocritical I just didn't get it. To me, from where I came from it wasn't real. What did I know about New York projects or Compton? It wasn't real but it was believable."

"But your take away from the music was all the negative stuff. The misogyny, the poverty, the violence."

"I wasn't trying to do that. If anything what happened was what I heard in the music reinforced what I was hearing all around me."

"And just like what you took from the music everything around you was all selective negativity."

"I didn't know no better. It wasn't even until I went into the military that I even had the chance to sit down and have a real conversation with a black person. So yeah maybe it was hypocritical but it wasn't intentional. So those racist people we were talking about earlier, I understand them, I understand why. So you have to give me credit for listening and changing the way I thought. I could have stayed ignorant and been a racist bastard like so many others. I could have taken from my youth and believed what I was being told even then. I mean I may have thought some aspects of black people were bad but I never thought the race as a whole were bad people. It might have been too late for you but it wasn't until those conversations, there in a bunk or in the mess hall in the military where some of my misconceptions were changed. To this day I still have lifelong friends who are black who I served with."

"So because you have black friends you're not racist?"

"I really hate when people say that. Just because you have one black friend doesn't mean you're not a racist. If you say that then you probably are and you probably think of that one black friend as an outlier. Me, I'm not racist because I don't think I'm any better than you. My skin color doesn't make me any better than you nor does it make you any better than me."

"Why? Why did you talk to black people once you joined the military?"

"I don't know. It wasn't some grandiose plan. I wasn't trying to learn about black people I was just talking to those going through the fire with me. It kind of happened organically but I didn't fight it like I could have. Man when you're life is on the line you don't care what the color the person next to you is or sex for that matter. Your only concern, at least mines I don't want to speak for others, my only concern was when the shit hits the fan will this person help me stay alive. Will they kill for me? It's a sobering thought but it's true. If need be will you shoot another man, kill him so we can go home?"

"So there are no racist people in the military?"

"I didn't say that. Of course there are. At every level. Sexist too. Homophobic. The same type of people you see out in the world, those same type of people live and work in the military. The public isn't perfect and neither is the military though I must say they are working hard to change."

"But they exist."

"Yes they exist and specifically about when talking about racists in the military, there are two types. Racists who came in racists, brainwashed before they showed up who only came to get military training to take back home when their enlistment is up. So they can build bunkers and plan for the apocalypse or join militias to taunt people they don't agree with."

"Black people."

"Everything is not always black and white. Yes black people but some of these people hate foreigners, they're anti-government, they're anti-Jew, they're anti-anything they don't agree with, they're anti-everything. And I don't mean just the ones in the military I mean the ones the military guys go home to. And the second type are those who still believe black people, and really any non-white males are not mentally capable of doing the job. They are the dangerous ones but they tend to be the older, longer enlisted soldiers. That tired way of thinking looks like is slowly fading away. They'll even make excuses for those non-white males who have risen through the ranks saying it is just for show. But like every category of people they are the minority. A miniscule minority but one is too many. The other group, the ones who came in that way, you'll never change their way of thinking no matter what. They're a lost cause. A cancer that should be removed from the military in my opinion."

"So shouldn't we as a nation be more concerned with these people, these people who want to bring the government down. Why aren't they talked about on all these news channels?"

"I don't make policy nor am I a program director. I was a soldier and now I'm a civilian."

"I never served. My father did. My uncle did. I have a few cousins in the service right now so we are a military family somewhat. So I'd first like to say thank you for your service. Though I know at some point today you will question the sincerity of what I just said know it is heartfelt. I never met them but I have two family members who never made it back home. They both died over there in Vietnam fighting a war to this day nobody can tell you what they died for? The only war this country has ever lost. Off topic but have you ever been to the monument?"

"The Vietnam Memorial, no I have not though I do plan on making it there one day. I want to see all the monuments to the dead soldiers of past wars not just Vietnam."

"I've been to it. Out of all the monuments, out of all the museums, out of all the architecture on the mall it is the most sombering to me. I know it is the not the intent but some of the others monuments seem to glorify war, to glorify dying in defense of your nation. And I'm not knocking dying for your nation and then your nation paying tribute to you, to their fallen but, I mean, I'm not trying to take anything away from the soldiers and their sacrifice"

"I know what you're trying to say but war sometimes is unavoidable. Yes the loss of life is tragic but"

"But sometimes necessary. I'm not knocking soldiers. I'm knocking decision makers. Sometimes war is necessary. But sometimes war is propaganda for the ruling but I really wasn't trying to go there. I was just trying to give credit to Vietnam War Memorial without knocking or discrediting the others. My original point was to me it seems different, feels like a tribute to the soldiers without it being a tribute to war if you know what I mean."

"I follow you."

"First there is this giant book, looks like old phone books if you remember what they look like."

"We're around the same age so yeah I remember phone books. My kids on the other hand would have no clue what you're talking about."

"Neither would mine. But when you're there the first thing you walk up to is this giant phone book full of names of the dead and where you can find them on the wall. Then you walk over to the wall itself. As you walk along the wall you descend down like you're going into this massive grave with these men and eight women who lost their lives."

"I didn't know there were any women inscribed on the wall."

"Neither did I until I looked it up once. Just curious one day. Googled it. You can find anything on google. But anyway. When you descend down along the wall the chaos and the noise and the people, everything around you sorta disappears. You can't see the street in front of you no more. You're no longer really aware of the people, the masses of people on the Mall behind you. It's just you, this massive black wall with all of its names and any others there paying tribute. You actually feel connected to the others, those touching the wall feeling the names, those grieving, those just paying their respects. Especially those who were there in Vietnam paying their respects to their fallen comrades, if you're lucky enough to meet one still alive willing to talk. It feels like when you are there you are there with their ghosts. When I was there I took a piece of paper, placed it over the names of the two family members I never had the opportunity to meet, the two who died over there. I took the piece of paper and I placed it over their names and I etched their names from the wall onto the paper. It was the most emotional thing I have ever done for someone else. When I got back home I gave the etchings to their living relatives, one wife, one brother. I can't even explain what if felt like at the monument and I wasn't in Vietnam. I could only imagine the feeling for those who were there, those who lived through it. I mean truthfully I can't imagine so like I said thank you for your service."

"Thank you! Now let me ask you a question just to change the subject before we break into tears here. To go back to what we were talking about earlier. What do you think as a black man yourself can be done to show black people in a more positive light?"

"That's a really good question. I'm going to break it down into two parts. What we black people can control and what is outside of our control. I'll start with what we can't control but you can. Non-black people and when I say black people I'm including all people of color so white people such as yourself the best thing you can do is what you already did. What you're doing right now. Get to know black people and change the narrative in your own mind. Don't just accept and believe the lazy stereotypes we are portrayed as. We as a community, as a group of people, we are more than just Oprah Winfrey, Will Smith and Michelle and Barak Obama and then the rest. Do you have an American Express card by any chance?"

"I do."

"Did you know Kenneth Chenault, a black man is or was the CEO of the company, even though I think if he hasn't yet he's retiring soon."

"I did not."

"But you know Bill Gates, Mark Zuckerberg and Steve Jobs, and Steve Jobs is dead. But you don't know Ursula Burns. You didn't even know the only black family in your town, not that you should have, they could have been far far away on the other side of town but you knew they existed. And to give you some credit here once you joined the military you changed and I applaud you for that because you didn't have to. You could have held onto your preconceived notions and had them harden and changed into lifelong prejudices but you didn't. You grew. That's what all people not just white people need to do. And when I say all people I mean black people too. We all need to talk to other cultures, other races, other people and judge them on an individual basis. But I can't make you or anyone else do that. That has to be an individual decision. You have to respect me enough not to judge me based on whatever it is your preconceived perception of me is. Now us, black people. We as a group of people, we need to stop supporting companies who don't support us. This is something hopefully we would also be joined in by other groups of people. Television and movies companies who don't hire people of color and women. Don't support them. Businesses who don't hire black people don't support them. We have to not buy their products, don't buy their movie tickets and don't watch their tv shows. Anything that portrays us in a negative and untrue light, we need to stop supporting them. When you call us monkeys we can't shop in your stores."

"You really think they were calling you monkeys? That had to be an honest mistake."

"No way was that an honest mistake. They put the black kid in a monkey hoodie and the white kid in a king hoodie. That ad had to go through several layers of okaying before it was used. They knew. Someone that okayed it knew. They just didn't think it was going to be this bad. You have to remember the marketing motto. No publicity is bad publicity. If that shirt would have said coolest cracker in the bag, do you think it would have ever seen the light of day. I don't even need you to answer because you know the answer. No."

"Coolest cracker in the bag. You have to admit that's funny. But you're right. But the not supporting stuff, hasn't that already started to a certain degree. Didn't the monkey company stocks drop? Movies like Ghost in the Shell and Noah. Weren't these movies boycotted because of their lack of diversity and didn't they bomb at the box office?"

"It wasn't just a lack of diversity. In those two cases it was an example of extreme cultural exploitation. How are you going to make a movie about a man from the Middle East, which is where Noah is from and not show that on the screen. Why does it always have to be white people portrayed as the saviors? And Ghost in the Shell. How are you going to take a Japanese anime, remake it, make all the characters Asian except the main character? Then get mad when people don't go and see it. Like we are supposed to go spend our money on that foolery. Like this white girl was supposed to be the savior of Japan. Come on now. And I'm not even knocking the Scarlett Johansen. She's crazy talented, a wonderful actress, and I can't blame her for taking the check but what did the producers and the movie studio expect. The backlash was immediate. So yeah it's happening somewhat but those movies are still getting greenlit and they are still being made."

"Don't you think they took that into account when they made the movie? Maybe they thought they could get a bigger audience that way? I'm just playing devil's advocate here."

"Then I'd say times are changing. Elizabeth Taylor couldn't play Cleopatra in today's times. And I'm not saying she didn't do a great job, I'm not saying Scarlett Johansen didn't do a great job in Ghost in the Shell or Tilda Swinton didn't do a great job in Dr. Strange because they did. What I'm saying is that is no longer acceptable, we can't let it be acceptable for a movie about Cleopatra and every Egyptian in the movie be played by actors and actresses who are lily white. How when they are African? Egypt has and always will be in Africa. Now Marc Antony and the Romans they can be played by white people. But Cleopatra, come on now. And this HBO show about an alternate history where the Confederate States won the Civil War and slavery is legal. How is something like that a good idea? Please tell me."

Silence

"And since we're on it have you ever read the description of Jesus in the Bible. His hair was like wool and His feet were bronze. Now I don't know of any white man who isn't mixed and has plenty of black or Middle Eastern DNA in him who has wooly hair and a bronze complexion. But that's the point, if they continue to make movies like this we have to continue not to pay to watch them, only watch them bomb. If they want to call us monkeys we can't support their business. If they don't want to employ us we can't support their business. If they don't want to employ us in senior roles we can't use their services. I wish we had a roll call of companies so we could look at their corporate structure and see how many decision makers are not white males."

"Why is Jesus' race or color important? Why isn't Who and What He is important?"

"I'll answer that like this. Why if it's not important do they not show him as depicted in the Bible? And what about all the other stuff I said after that?"

"I don't have a problem with that stuff except the issue of companies corporate hiring. They want to hire the best people. If the best people are all white people then so be it."

"It's about opportunity. There are tons of qualified non-white males who are competent and qualified that never get a chance. I don't want to support you if my brother can't get a fair opportunity. And pay attention, have you ever noticed it's only the people who have something in their possession who question its importance? Jesus in all the pictures is white so white people say why is it important? Businesses with all white boards say why is it important? But the truth of the matter is we have way more important issues than the color of Jesus. If you believe in Jesus you believe in Jesus. His color won't get you to Heaven but the change of His image is just another whitening of the world. Soon we're going to see pictures of Dr. King as a white man."

Quick laugh.

"It's not funny I'm serious."

"I wasn't laughing at the gist of what you were saying but Dr. King being presented as a white man, c'mon that's never going to happen."

"What's stopping them? They already don't teach his story in some places, see where you grew up. History is a narrative and the narrative is controlled by those in power. They don't say the library is where the lies are buried for no reason."

"Who says that?"

"You've never heard that saying before?"

"Nope."

"Interesting. But let's go back to what you asked a few seconds ago.
What can be done to show black people in a more favorable light? We
just have to be shown in truth. They only show us when we do something
wrong. They don't show us when we do something right. At least not in
the amounts they show white people doing good. I always wanted to ask
a news producer how they pick and choose what stories make the air and
I wonder if he would give an honest answer."

"Or she."

"You're right. Or she. And to answer the rest of your question, for
something we can do ourselves, we need to stop spending money on the
nonsense. You don't have a house but you have a fifty thousand dollar
car you're paying way too much for every month. We need to get our
own house in order as a community. But even more we as a people need
to give back and pull each other up. Harvard has a thirty six billion dollar
endowment fund. Howard University with all its prestigious alumni has
something somewhere between a million and nothing. People leave our
communities and never look back. For those in dire straits, and this refers
to all poor people not just black people but poor white people, poor
whoever, we have to learn education is the way out. There are no
shortcuts. Every person who's made it that you think made it overnight
put in a lot of hard work and long hours you never see. Every athlete,
every musician, every entrepreneur, every person who came from
nothing. We have to go through the struggle. Nobody wants to struggle
anymore. Everyone wants instant fame and money. Since we have very
few to look up at we think there is no way out. We need to change our

mindset. Now don't get me wrong there are plenty who are doing it but we need to do it better."

"Man this is funny, not ha ha funny but funny coincidental. I was just having this conversation with a buddy of mine the other day. I'm glad you said not just black people but all poor people. We weren't talking about black people but we were talking about where we grew up and the poverty we grew up in and how we pulled ourselves out from underneath it. I hear people talking about the rose that grew from the concrete. Cool. It takes an amazing person to be able to do that but I didn't grew up much different. I grew from death. We didn't even have concrete there. All we had was dirt. And dirt where nothing grew, no flowers, no bugs, not even no weeds. Nothing grew there. Try to plant a flower it died in its seed so I know struggle. It's not reserved for only black people. And once people realize the real problem isn't white versus black it's the poor versus the rich then we can start to fix it. Everyone in this country has an opportunity. If you want to educate yourself it can be done. If you want to do something it can be done. It might not be easy and it probably won't happen overnight, in fact it'll probably take years but it can be done. But you're right though. Nobody wants to struggle. No one wants to put in the work. And I shouldn't say no one because like you said there are plenty of people who put in the time, the blood, the sweat and the tears to get what they want but way too many are ok not putting in the effort then complaining about it."

"But the media doesn't show the people like yourself who made it out. A nice house doesn't get eyes drawn to the screen. A house up in flames does."

"You're absolutely right there. You know somewhere the once tried to have a positive news show on tv and no one watched it. No one wanted to hear everything was going great."

"My point exactly."

"But know it's not the media's duty to teach. They're job is to report. And the crazy thing is once you look at it, it's not their job to report both sides. Their job is to report factually, well it used to be their job to report factually at least."

"Keep going I'm listening."

"Let's take the two biggest news tv services out there. Fox news and CNN. Fox news panders to the Republican side of the news and CNN to the Democratic side. Can we agree on that there?"

"Keep going."

"Why don't they show the other side of a story? I'll tell you why. Because it's tv. And tv isn't run by the truth. Television is a business that's why your favorite tv shows get cancelled. And the business of television including news program is run by advertisements. You get more money from the same advertisements the bigger your audience is. Neither Fox News nor CNN is going to change the dynamic of what its reporting because its audience doesn't want to hear the other side. They may turn off the station if they did. Less eyes means less money, less advertising money. You know the saying. Money is the root of all evil. But it's our fault as people too. We don't turn into our favorite news channels to hear the truth. We turn in to hear what we want to hear. We want the news media to pander and cater to us or else we wouldn't listen. We don't want a balanced news program because we don't want to hear what someone else thinks. And pander they do."

"How?"

"Like this. If I was to say this city arrested 50,000 people on drug charges but this suburb arrested 500 people on drug charges you would think that city had a way bigger drug problem than that suburb or that tiny town. Am I right?"

"Numbers don't lie and that is a wide margin 50,000 to 500."

"Ok. But if I said the city of 1,000,000 residents had 50,000 arrests and the suburb of 10,000 residents had 500 arrests then what would you think?"

"You'd think the same. 50,000 arrests is a lot."

"See, that's what they know, a lot of people listen but we don't all really pay attention. If you look at both sets of numbers 5% of the population got arrested for drugs. It's just that the suburb, since it is only 1% the size of the city, the numbers look worse. Now if they were to have said both in the city and in the suburb 5% of the people were arrested because of drugs you would have had a different reaction. You wouldn't have thought of the city as so bad."

"Interesting."

"We need to stop taking for granted what is said and believing everything that is being fed to us. Especially when watching the news listen and pay attention. Then these news shows use those numbers to prove a point. Oh black people this or white people this or the city this. When in actuality it's all the same."

"So what about social media?"

"That's a joke too. All these social media platforms use algorithms to give you stories they think you want to see. They blind you to the other side, to different views and opposite ways of thinking. Like what happened with the election."

Rubs his hands together. "I've been waiting to talk about this."

"May I ask who you voted for?"

"In the primary I voted for Bernie Sanders."

"So you're a democrat?"

"Yes I'm a democrat."

"So since Bernie Sanders lost who did you vote for in the general election?"

"In the general election I voted, begrudgingly, and believe me it took all I had to actually push the button but I voted for Hillary Clinton."

"Why do you say begrudgingly?"

"I know a lot of people love her but not me. I didn't want to vote for her. Even though I thought she'd do a decent job as President and it would have been great to finally have a woman president it was something about her, the way she handled herself that I didn't like. I didn't like the way she thought she deserved to be President, like it was her right. I don't know if she really believed that or not but that's the way she came off to me. She didn't go out and fight for it. She didn't take a stand. Then being a Bernie Sanders supporter I didn't like the way the whole thing with him was handled. Even before we knew the truth it seemed like the establishment of the Democrats didn't want him to win. And then you know what, we all learned later that was exactly the case. Then even after she defeated Bernie in the primaries she didn't court his followers she just assumed that his statement of support for her, which seemed forced, it just seemed like she thought that was good enough to get his votes and for me it wasn't."

"But you voted for her so it was good enough."

"I did. But a lot of people who would have voted for Bernie, a lot of black people especially didn't vote at all. Back then nobody liked Trump and his rhetoric. Nobody thought he was a vile a human being as his is. Even though people thought it might happen, people hoped the hate he spoke was all bluster so people decided not to vote at all which swung the election Trump's way. Almost any other democrat would have trounced Trump but in my opinion her arrogance did her in."

"Can you call him President Trump?"

"He has the job but until he represents the country for all Americans I will never call him that. My not calling him president doesn't take away from having the job so why does it matter?"

"You called him vile but didn't he stand in front of the nation and call for unity?"

"He did. But what he says and what he does are two separate things. A man can't call for unity then ask to build a wall. A man can't call for unity then take away protections for the country's most needy. But he won so hey we have to deal with it."

"Weren't black people offended when white people said Obama wasn't my President, when they wouldn't say President Obama?"

"Yes we were! But the difference is Obama didn't do anything wrong except be black. I know too many people who have family from those shithole countries Trump talked about. Those countries where everyone has ADIS. But he won, and they're not going to impeach him so it doesn't matter. When it could have mattered we didn't step up so I can't blame him for basking in it."

"So you really think Hillary would have been a better President than Trump?"

"We'll never know will we. Like I said I had my reservations about Hillary Clinton. But also, even though I believe he was an excellent President"

"Whoa. He. Wait, before the words come out your mouth, how can you say he was an excellent President? Are we talking about Bill here?"

"I was about to. And before you cut me off there was a but coming."

"Is this about what he did to Monica Lewinsky?"

"No. He cheated on his wife, so what. Trump slept with a porn star then paid her off. He's on his third wife. I could care less. There's innuendo out there it's him sleeping with Russian prostitutes that's in that dossier the UK spy made though we may never know. But me personally none of that matters. Didn't JFK have an affair with Marilyn Monroe? Means nothing to me."

"It doesn't show you anything about their character?"

"It does. And I know I'm in the minority when it comes to this topic but cheating on your wife is so rampant I stopped caring especially when it comes to politicians. That's between him and his wife not me. Are you going to be a good, whatever you're running for? If you're running for re-election I would not care I'd look at your record. It you're new it might sway me. It would probably sway me so I guess it does matter in some cases. Plus so many of these politician's cheat on their wives. Or they trade them in for younger models. Clinton, one of the most vocal republicans asking for his impeachment was found about a year later to have been cheating on his wife. So you see why I could care less. Let them disclose all the cheating and sexual abuse scandals that's buried in that Washington dirt then maybe I'll care. You and I both know good men and women who were unfaithful to their spouses. Shoot, which pastor is it going to be today? For me that's between you, your spouse and God. Are these people good bosses, good employees, good neighbors? What happens in a person's home relationship wise is between them. You'll never know what's really going on so I put little stock in it. Now if I was his wife then he might die but I'm not so hey, I never comment on another man's household."

"That's hypocritical."

"It is. But what's even more hypocritical is talking about Bill Clinton's past and demonizing him when Trump is doing it presently and we're trying to excuse it. If you're going to kill one, and I'm talking to both sides here, you need to acknowledge and kill the other the same way. If it's wrong then they are both wrong. Now we all know all Bill wanted to do was smoke weed, cheat and play his sax. But the difference is he wanted a peaceful world to do it in. Now to do that he had to make sure the economy was good and it was great during his eight years and he wasn't looking to start a war. He wasn't prodding countries with nukes to start a war with nuclear fallout. But, here's the but I was talking about. The problem a lot of black people have with Hillary's husband was Bill Clinton locked up a lot of black people during his Presidency. And they were forced to serve long sentences that clearly weren't appropriate to the crimes they committed. They were severe and disproportionate compared to the sentences of white offenders during the same time period."

"But crimes were committed weren't they. If they did the crime then don't complain about doing the time."

"Yes they were. You are absolutely right. But let's take a look at now versus then. This is a microcosm of the unfairness of America and its hypocriticalness when it comes to black people. Then there was 'The War on Drugs.' Crack to be specific. It was an epidemic. No question about it crack was destroying neighborhoods and families. It was the Wild West during those times. Young black men left and right were being arrested and thrown in jail and given sentences with crazy numbers."

"Deservedly so. They were selling drugs. They were breaking the law. I have no sympathy for them."

"Remember you said those words deservedly so. Alright. Crack exploded on the scene and became an epidemic the country over, am I right?"

"Yes you are."

"You need cocaine to make crack. Who was bringing the cocaine into the country? These kids weren't growing it in their backyards, concrete backyards. Can't grow the plants there. So who were they buying the cocaine from? How was the drugs getting in the country and to these kids? And now, how does drugs get into prisons. It isn't the prisoners bringing the stuff in. But back to then, the crack years. We know President Reagan and The FBI brought drugs into these neighborhoods to support and fund the Contras in Nicaragua. But none of these people got arrested. Not a single person. Just low level sellers. How is that fair? How many policemen and Federal agents took payouts to get the drugs through? How many custom agents? How many of those people were arrested in comparison? How many businessman, lawyers, banks and bankers laundering the money got rich off the backs of these kids selling drugs? Look at Miami. A whole city was built off the drug game. Miami then wasn't Miami now. It wouldn't be the resort destination it is without that era. But we only focused on arresting these black kids."

"You called it a game. Those kids didn't know the rules to the game they were playing. And the rules clearly state pawns get sacrificed by the king for the king. I'm a soldier, I know. It's not fair but life's not fair and they still, no matter how you want to spin it, they still committed a crime? Even if others got away with it. If the feds and the cops and bankers and lawyers would have gotten caught I would have no sympathy for them either."

"You're right. When it's black people, black kids, its lock them up they committed a crime, even if they were only pawns. Let me say when it's black people 'cause not all of those who were locked up were kids. So black people. But let me ask you, what's the drug epidemic right now? What are all the commercials trying to bring awareness to and prevention for now?"

"Right now I'd say heroin."

"I agree. The epidemic drug of right now is heroin. So why is there no war on heroin? Why aren't we locking up en masse low-level sellers of heroin as we did crack? Or when meth was the epidemic? I didn't see a war on meth and meth is still ruining lives out there. Or pills. Next to heroin pills is probably the most dangerous thing on the street right now. But we don't see mass arrests for those things. We don't see it flashed on the news every day. Heroin right now is killing people and neighborhoods like crack did but I don't see roundups of people. Why? Could it be because the low-level sellers of heroin aren't black kids from the hood? And don't say it's not as bad because it is because in Philly, where it's not even as bad as it in in some states like Ohio, in Philly they want to open a storefront or something of the nature where they can provide a 'safe' place for people to shoot up peacefully so they can be protected. This is the city government that wants to do this not the people of the city spearheading this movement. Really? Really!? So you're going to allow them to use illicit and illegal drugs legally. Why not lock them up? Why aren't they 'deservedly' going to jail? Aren't they breaking the law?"

"Maybe it's because as a nation we learned it wasn't right? That there is a better way of handling drug epidemics and that locking people up is not the solution to the answer."

"Then why wasn't that your answer a few seconds ago. A few seconds ago it was they committed a crime they 'deserved' to go to jail. Do you see what I'm getting at? Having tons of black kids locked up doesn't bother you, it doesn't resonate with you because you're not affected by it. But if it was tons of white kids that would hit home. And let's be real here the heroin epidemic is hitting white people harder than black people. So they can lock up black kids for selling and using drugs but white kids get a pass now? Why did the thought process change? Why aren't they deservedly so going to jail en masse? Where's the outrage? Where's the Congressional hearings, the drug czars? It's different when it's suburban white America? You think they are going to lock up a generation of white kids?"

Pause

"This is also why I didn't want to vote for Hillary. Would we go back to that? She didn't say to her husband then that it was wrong."

"Maybe because it wasn't wrong. The people that got locked up committed a crime. That's why they were arrested and convicted. Now maybe the penalties weren't handed out equally and yes a ton of people got away with a lot of stuff but that doesn't absolve those that committed the crime of the crime. Your combining two different things. Yes the court system is prejudiced against black people but don't get yourself into the system and you don't have to worry about it being fair. And that was then. Hopefully we've learned from those mistakes as a country and moved on. So why didn't you vote for Trump? This is exactly the stuff he is fighting for."

"Trump isn't going to fighting for black kids. And he, unless your living under a rock or believe the lies he's selling, he aint fighting for white kids either unless their parents are rich. That's the only people Trump is fighting for. Rich people. Is that who you voted for?"

"Yes."

"Why?"

"You first. Why was it you didn't vote for him? Was it because he was a Republican? Have you ever voted for a Republican?"

"Have you ever voted for a Democrat?"

"I'll answer but you first."

"Have I ever voted for a Republican? Yes. Not often. Maybe only once. And to be truthful it was only because the Democratic opponent was terrible, and I mean terrible. I'll tell you a quick story. I was in DC when they re-elected Marion Barry. The same Marion Barry who was caught on tape smoking crack with an ex-girlfriend. The same Marion Barry who did a terrible job running the city but they loved him for some reason, some inexplicable reason that I'll never understand. I guess you had to be from down there to understand why and I wasn't so I didn't. Anyway, at that moment I decided I wouldn't vote for someone just because a politician was the same race, because he was a man, or she was a woman, had done the job before, none of that. But I do vote for Democrats because they align more with my thinking than Republicans. At least what they say."

"So you don't think they mean what they say?"

Laughs. "These politicians take more money than anybody, pay for play. Not all of them but way too many of them. These people are the most crooked people on earth. And the federal politicians, they fight with each other in public then they all go to the same country clubs and smoke Cuban cigars, cigars that were illegal to the rest of the country but they have them. They drink their fine cognac and cheat on their wives. Not all mind you but enough and way too many."

"I still don't understand the anti-Republican bias you have. Republicans are the party that freed the slaves. They are the party of Lincoln."

"In history only. Lincoln wouldn't have elected Donald Trump. That part of the Republican Party is long gone. What they did in the past has no bearing on what they are doing in the present because the people, those old Republicans who did those things you reference, they are all long dead and gone. Today the Republican Party is the party of the rich. I once was five years old and thought like a child. I'm not five anymore. So have you ever voted for a democrat?"

"No. Why should I. That don't represent me or what I stand for. So what's your problem with Trump? If you really didn't want to vote for Clinton why not vote for Trump?"

"Where should I start? Ok first, if it wasn't Trump there were a few Republicans I might have actually voted for. Not Cruz, not Christie, and definitely not Ben Carson. Yes the black man would not have voted for the black man. Unlike you by your own admission, I was actually paying attention to both sides. Now before you say anything yes it would have taken a lot for me to vote republican but I actually thought about it. Now why not Trump let's start here. Give me one second and let me pull it up. This is his quote to black people while campaigning. And I quote 'You're living in poverty, your schools are no good, you have no jobs, 58% of your youth is unemployed, what the hell do you have to lose?' What the hell do I have to lose? He wasn't courting black votes. He didn't care about black votes and he doesn't to this day care about black people. I'm not living in poverty. Second your schools are no good. Aren't public schools everybody's schools. If so then why are public schools in black communities no good? Are they deliberately underfunding them? That is the problem with today's society. We are so fractured we don't care about anything else. First rule of war is divide and conquer and Trump has America at its most divided since slavery. He is the wedge and the hammer pushing the split wider. And his daddy was a member of the klan."

"Even if his dad was that doesn't mean he is."

"Theoretically maybe but his housing practices in his buildings say he had the same racist train of thought. It's all public record. Look at the lawsuits. Look at the New York cases of discrimination filed against him. Does that sound like someone who cares about black people? He didn't even want their money. I don't know how much more racist it gets than that. Does that sound like someone who wants my vote, who is courting my vote? Why? Because he knew he would do nothing to help the black community and it shows. He hasn't done one thing to help since being elected."

"That's not the President's job."

"Of course it's his job. At its very basic the President is supposed to make life better for All Americans. Emphasis on the All. Listen this guy doesn't' care a lick. He has or had two black people in his staff. Omarosa, somebody who most black people want to throw off the black island, who did nothing of any substance during her time in the White House. You don't go from the White House to the Big Brother House?"

"You sound like that Dave Chappelle skit."

Snicker. "Yeah she wouldn't get drafted by anyone. And the other, I don't know her name but she was his son's wedding planner and he made her a Regional Director for HUD which oh my fault, I forgot about the third, HUD is helmed by the third black person, Ben Carson. Whom you haven't heard a word from since he got the post."

"Why are you mad at the wedding planner lady? She was given an opportunity. Aint that what you want for black people?"

"She didn't deserve nor have the qualifications for the position. Now if I was her I wouldn't have turned it down either let's be serious, I'll take the check too but she should have never been given that position. It's an old trick. Give someone who is going to fail the job then say look I gave a black person a chance and see what happened they failed."

"So he's hired black people, maybe not a lot but what do you expect. He's far from racist."

"Just because he hired a couple of tokens for show, people with no chance of actually doing anything positive in their positions, doesn't mean he cares about black people as a whole. Like I said just do dome research on him and his hiring practices and his business practices and its blatant how he discriminates against black people. Those three are just for show say he can look I do have black people like they are some kind of accessory. How many times has he been sued for discrimination? Multiple times. With once being too many. And moving on, thirdly. He said and again I quote 'It's like a magnet. Just kiss. I don't even wait. And when you're a star, they let you do it. You can do anything. Grab 'em by the pussy. You can do anything.' He said he can just grab 'em by the pussy. He just admitted to sexual not misconduct he admitted to sexual violence. And don't say that's locker room talk. I've been in plenty of locker rooms and no one has ever said anything like that, ever. We don't just take it. That's what rapists say. He's just vile and disgusting. Now maybe that's what powerful white men who think they rule the world say in their private clubs but don't put that on the locker room. So let me ask you why would I vote for someone who thinks like that? I have a daughter. If anyone ever just grabbed her by the pussy I might end up in jail on a murder charge. But you, you folks overlooked all of that. I couldn't. Even though I didn't want to vote for Clinton, in my mind she was the clear better of the two evils with Hillary being bad but Trump being more like the Devil. Maybe not the Devil because there is only one Devil but he sure is the Devil's Advocate. Matter fact he's worse than that he's the Devil's Proxy. And at least Sean Spicer left, quit or got fired or whatever but Sarah Sanders, Trump's the Devil's Proxy and Sarah Huckabee Sanders, she's Viceroy to the Devil's Proxy."

"That was mean. What does Mrs. Sanders have to do with any of this?"

"She repeats the lies. Over and over again. And then she tries to quantify them and rationalize them and say they're not lies. They're alternative facts. I know she didn't coin the phrase the other one, Kellyanne Conway, who you don't even see anymore, the put your feet on the couch in the Oval office did but the Viceroy she's runs with it. Everything is fake news. No they are not alternative facts and it is not fake news. What Trump says out is mouth are outright lies. He's told over fifteen hundred lies in less than a year in office. I wish I was exaggerating the number but I'm not look it up. And let's not try and downplay them and call them untruths, Trump speaks in bald faced lies and Ms. Sanders pie baking skills can't hide the fact that she okays them and even justifies him. And it's not just her. Because he holds the office others try to defend this guy. He called Africa and Haiti shithole countries. If he's bad enough to say it be bad enough to own it. Don't lie and say you didn't. Two senators one republican and one democrat both admitted it but others oh I don't recall. Bullshit you recall. They're just enabling him. Or the one who said he said shithouse, like shithouse is better than shithole c'mon. That's why I call her that. She's the Devil's Proxy's Viceroy. Sanders is the first one to stand in front of the camera, in front of the nation, and try to defend the nonsense, tries to okay the lies like the American people are stupid. She's just as bad. You voted for the guy. Why? And how do you rationalize the job he has done or do you?"

"I voted for him for one simple reason. I believe him to be a Christian man who would go to Washington and clean it up. I thought for me personally he would make America better. Point blank simple and plain. I voted for him because I believe in his Christian values and secondly because I believed he would make the country safe."

"If you believe Donald Trump to believe in those Christian values he says he does I have some land under the ocean I want to sell you. This is the same guy who didn't know it's pronounced Second Thessalonians and not two Thessalonians. Maybe if you watch his actions and not his words you'll see clearer. And if anything during our conversation I hope you've learned nothing is simple and plain. Nothing. Not one single thing. There's always nuances to things, angles you didn't or couldn't see before. And this guy totally blinded you because he said he wasn't a politician.

Because he said he was a businessman. He told you he was a Christian but his acts are so unchristian like it borders on insanity. And Christians excuse his behavior. They villainize others but defend him."

"How can you doubt another person's Christianity? You have no idea what he believes in his heart."

"You're right I don't. I have no idea what's in his heart. But his actions go against every core value of the Bible. How many commandments has he broken? People like him give Christians a bad rap. He may be a Christian by belief but his walk is that of the devil."

"We all have fallen short so why do you judge him?"

"Because he holds the job. And because he uses his platform to divide and to lie. Lies he can't admit to. And he has never asked for forgiveness. Why? Because he doesn't believe in the words that come out his mouth. Even Lucifer knows the words in the Bible."

"And just so you know he hasn't blinded anyone. He's done exactly what he said he would do."

"And what's that build a wall and ban Muslims."

"Yes."

"So you're ok with him banning Muslims just because they're Muslims, because of their faith?"

"Yes. It's a violent religion."

"So you agree it is a ban on Muslims and not whatever spin he's trying to put on it?"

"No doubt. I'm not going to sit here and insult your intelligence of course it is a ban on Muslims. And they should be banned because their religion espouses violence."

"Have you ever looked into Islam as a religion?"

"No, why should I?"

"So a religion you know nothing about except what you've been told is a violent religion. And you want this wall built? A wall Trump said Mexico would pay for but now he wants us, the American public to pay for. A wall that will do no good except feed into the myth of security and please white Americans who don't want people of color in the country. Let's call it what it is."

"Now you're wrong. The wall will keep out illegals from crossing the border."

"One it won't. Look at what every non-politician says about the effects of a wall. Why are you people so afraid of letting in people of color into this country?"

"First stop with the you people stuff. If I said that you'd be insulted. I'm me I don't speak for everyone."

"You're right. My apologies. So do you think white America, the white America who doesn't want immigration from brown and black countries, could the reason why be because this country was stolen from the Native Americans? You know the ones the football team in DC calls redskins?"

"You have a problem with everything don't you?"

"I have a problem with everything that's wrong and no matter how you spin in that name is racist."

"You know I'm not from DC?"

"Not the point."

"Well what is your point?"

"My point is, America, this land we live on is stolen. Your ancestors raped and pillaged the people who rightfully belong on these lands. White people are always talking about our country this and our country that and we can't have immigration to this country, a country was stolen at the point of a gun. So every time I hear a white person say this is my country in that context, in a context where they want to exclude people I laugh. It is not. Is that why white people don't want people of color coming to this country? Are you afraid if enough people of color come to America, if that happens and once white people are a minority in this country the same will happen to you? You will lose your land, land that is not your land. That this won't be yours anymore. Are you afraid of the Redskins, and the brown skins, and the black skins, and some of your own white skins who don't lean racist?"

"Even with your incendiary comments, yes that happened, the Indians lost their land but I didn't do it. My ancestors didn't do it. And if you want to be real they lost. War was brought to them and the Indians, they lost. To the victor go the spoils. Is that what you want to hear? The Indians lost."

"Can we stop calling them Indians. They are not Indians. Columbus and crew thought they were in India so they called them Indians. They are Americans, more American than any of us."

"You're right but like I said they lost. Then the civil war happened and the south lost. When war comes there can only be one victor."

"So is white America afraid that war is coming for them, karma?"

"No. Not at all. Like I said they lost. The south lost. So it is what it is. In Africa there were wars and the losing tribes, there men were sold off to European slave traders to be shipped to America and sold as slaves. None of this is of my making just like black people being sold into slavery by their own people in Africa is not of my making nor is it of yours. Man I'm just trying to live my life with the hands I was dealt in the best country in the world."

"You know more history than you let on. You're right though. African blacks sold their enemies to the white man and into American slavery. Even then we weren't united. It's always been a problem. So relax. I don't blame you. I just want you to acknowledge you're living off the fruits of that ill-conceived labor."

"I do realize that but we're here to talk about the here and now. There is nothing I can do or say about happened before me. But this President's wall will keep us safe. Forget the history look at the present. Look at the drugs and violence and poverty that is coming from down there up here. It's already hard enough to make a living without more people coming who need a living made for them."

"Nobody needs a living made for them. People just want to work and feed their families, same as the people who want to come to this country. And you know you can be against illegal immigration and be against a wall, a wall that won't work keeping anyone out. But let's say it would work. Even if a wall would work, which it won't, it's only going to keep those people out from South of the border. Again people of color. Brown people from South America. What about the northern border. You don't want to build a wall there. Why is it that Canadians can come and go into and out of this country as they so choose? Is it because historically this country doesn't care about white people coming and going? I'm just asking. And did you know more drugs come across the northern border than the southern? And through both coasts but we're not building walls there. But let's agree to disagree for now, even though you're on the wrong side of facts here, let's continue. What has this president actually achieved, what has he done?"

"He's changed the tax code to make it simpler and better for businesses like mine. Like he said he would."

"Ok. He's changed the tax code to put more money in the pockets of people who already have money. How is that helping? As a business owner how much of that money are you going to put back into your people? And when I mean your people I mean are you going to give across the board raises to your employees or even hire more employees because of the new tax law? Or are you going to go the PR route and say you're going to give your employees bonuses knowing very few of your employees actually meet the criteria for the bonuses?"

"I'm not do anything. And I'm definitely not giving anyone across the board raises. Raises at my place of business are based on production and results. Nobody gets anything just because. Work hard like I did and earn your raise. I'm not giving anybody anything more just because I might have more to give. Earn more and you get more. I built this business not them. But truly I don't even know how much more money my business will save. First before anything I have to figure that out, what the difference will be before I do anything. I really have no idea right now. If there is a substantial amount of savings then I will reinvest some of it in the company, hopefully growing it then yes hiring more people."

"But only if the savings are substantial. What would you consider substantial. You don't have to answer that I'm not trying to get into your finances, but if the amount is not substantial what will you do with it?"

"Honestly. Pocket it. What else can I do with it? It is money I earned, it is money due to me. It is my business. Do you see something wrong with that?"

"No I don't, not at all. I find no blame or fault in what you just said. It just proves my point. Money doesn't trickle down. People with money just get bigger bank accounts to hold it all. Now what I do find blame and fault in is the fact that the way this tax reform was always framed was a way to spur the economy and a way to put money back into the pockets of the middle class. And it raised the deficit we are always hearing must be cut by not millions, not billions, but trillions. But when it comes to social services oh there is no money. And by your own admission the savings aren't going to be passed down to the people who need it, that's not going to happen unless the savings are substantial. Now be honest who from this tax plan makes out the best?"

"The richer you are the better you make out. It's obvious to anyone paying attention. But that's not just his tax plan that is with everything in life. But you can't blame those who have for achieving a level of success and wanting to reap the benefits. I worked my business from the ground, from nothing to what it is now. It was my ass on the line if it failed no one else's. I would have been the one homeless. Me. I'm self-made. I deserve this benefit. I write the checks. You want to be a boss, I'm all for it then you can make the rules, until then."

"No one is self-made. You have employees right?"

"Of course."

"And those employees at its most basic are implementing your strategy, your business idea to help bring your business to profit. You couldn't handle every duty of your business as a one man operation am I right?"

"You are right at its most basic. But like you said nothing is basic or simple. If my business fails I lose everything. If I start to lose money my employees they still get paid. I still have to pay the bills. It's my asset on the line."

"And if your asset loses money the first thing you do is start firing people. Do you think your employees want to be out on the job market looking without a job? You know it's always easier to get a job when you have one already. Do you think your employees want to be without a paycheck? Don't get me wrong I know you write the checks. And yes in the beginning you laid the foundation. But right now you're sleeping on the top floor of a house your employees keep adding floors to. An architect is only an artist without someone to build his building. It may be his vision but he's not welding steel girders together. That's all I'm saying."

"But here's the thing, most of my employees are replaceable. I'm not. It's my name on the marquee. If they want it they can build their own with their own name in lights. Listen, I hope they do. I hope we all make it though you and I both know that won't happen. Every one of my employees have not only the opportunity to grow and move up but also the ability to leave at any point. If they find better they leave as they should. But I can't. They can go wherever they want or do what I did. Be a boss and start their own business. Go to school learn to be an executive."

"Every CEO is replaceable. There plenty of smart people in the world. But I understand this is your baby. No one will run it like you."

"Damn skippy!"

"So other than make rich people richer what else has Trump done. Has he done anything to the benefit of the American people as a country as a whole?"

"He's keeping us safe."

"From what?"

"From the jihad Muslims."

"I forgot that fast you think that. You're smoking the sticky-icky aren't you?"

"Why do you say that?"

"How is he keeping us safe?"

"One he wants to build a wall but they won't let him. Two he's keeping the Muslims who want to kill Americans out the country."

"Man you are brainwashed aren't you. Have you ever met a Muslim, an American Muslim, a foreign Muslim?"

"No I haven't."

"You were in the military, you never met a Muslim in the military?"

"I mean probably I have but they weren't friends of mine."

"But they were soldiers?"

"Yes, there are Muslims in our military. And yes, they are good soldiers."

"Maybe the same way you had conversations with black people you should have conversations with a few Muslims. You're a Christian man am I right to say that? You've said you are am I right?"

"Yes you are and proud to be. And I didn't avoid Muslims in the military I just didn't serve with any or at least any that I knew of."

"Do you know I'm a Christian man also?"

"No I didn't. How was I supposed to know that? And what does it matter in regard to Muslims. Their Qur'an tell them to kill non-believers."

"That's why I asked have you ever met any Muslims. Because all your information is from what you're being told. And it's not an accurate portrayal of who they are. Like I said I'm a Christian man myself. I do not believe what Muslims believe but I believe they are people first and deserve to be treated as such."

"Not after 9/11."

"Because you need to be safe?"

"I need this whole country to be safe. Including you and your family."

"So you're ok with excluding, ostracizing, and fear mongering against an entire set of people because they don't believe what you believe."

"If it keeps Americans safe then yes."

"What if it doesn't? What if the only reason behind the façade of safety is because they are different? I know Muslims. There are a lot of Muslim people here in this city. And they are good decent non-violent people. How many people died in 9/11?"

"Around three thousand. Three thousand Americans were killed for no other reason than because they were Americans. They were targeting our monetary system because they were, are jealous of our wealth."

"Outside of 9/11 how many Americans on American soil have been killed by foreign Muslims?"

"I don't know, how many?"

"None. Not a single one."

"That means what we as a country are doing is working. That means the ban is working."

"That means what we are doing was working before Trump instituted his ban which like you admitted to is a Muslim ban."

"Oh it's definitely a ban on Muslims, but it's a ban for the safety of the American people. Trump can call it whatever he wants because he has to, to keep it in place."

"So if safety is the key then why are we not banning white American men for the safety or the nation? Or men in general?"

"Because men aren't a threat to our National security."

"I knew you would say that and I knew this would come up so I checked the statistics before I came, just to make sure I got them right. In America 98% of all mass shooting and 90% of murders are committed by men. So why are we not banning all men from the country, you know, to keep us safe. Let's throw us all out so our women and children can be safe. Then they can allow back in who they want, you know pick and choose."

"You're being ridiculous."

"No. I'm using the same logic you're regurgitating, the same logic they are using in their ban. Muslims are the so-called problem so you want to ban Muslims. But in America the real problem are men so why not ban men."

"You can't ban all men."

"I'll continue. 9/11 was perpetrated by a group of Muslims so we must ban all Muslims or so the logic goes no matter how illogical it is. So let's take a look at the data. Over the past thirty five years 64% of mass shooting were committed by white men. 16% by black men. All mass shootings were committed by American citizens. That leaves 20% by non-black or white men, women, and children such as school shootings. Since 9/11 the two most deadly mass shootings happened in Las Vegas and Orlando. One was committed by a man who was a radical Islamist. He killed 49 people and wounded 53 in the Orlando nightclub. And the other was committed by a white man who killed 200 people and wounded 50 more in Las Vegas shooting up a concert. And let's not forget about the Nazi wannabe, another white man who ran over 19 people in Charlottesville. So if we are going to protect the nation from Muslims who may be terrorists in the name of security why are we not protecting the country from white men who may also be terrorists? White men have committed more terroristic crimes on American soil than any other group of people ever. But we're not banning white men, Christian white men mostly. And while I'm at it one last thing about 9/11. Why are black people always told to forget about slavery, it happened so long ago, we're past that but every day its remember 9/11. Never forget 9/11. Is it because maybe they want to keep it fresh in your mind so they can scare you into a Muslim ban?"

"Your numbers are all good but statistics can be manipulated to agree with the person presenting them. I could find numbers that counter everything your saying."

"Find them then. Show me." Pause. "Understand I'm not for banning white people. I love white people as I love all people. My friends look like those Benneton ads. I love everybody. Understand I'm not blaming you personally or your race as a whole for the crimes of a small group. I'm not afraid of you nor any other white person. But that is what this Muslim ban is. It's fear mongering. But if you're going to put it into place then don't let any white men in because the data will tell you white men have a greater propensity towards mass violence than any other group. We as a country, if we wanted to secure it we should be more concerned with white men than anybody else, so says the data not the fear mongering. And white boys. Every mass school shooing has been perpetrated by a white male juvenile but you don't hear me saying let's ban all white kids because they might shoot up a school. Sounds crazy right. Now you know how this ban sounds to those who actually thought it through and weren't being pulled by their puppet strings."

"You make a good point then you take it too far with the unnecessary comment. It invalidates the point you're trying to make. Makes you sound like you have no clue about what you're talking about."

"That last comment was to make you think. Who's pulling your strings? Who's leading you down the path and why? But back to Trump. What else has he done? He tried to eliminate the America Cares Act."

"No he didn't. What's the America Cares Act?"

"You don't even know what it is but you're saying he didn't."

"Because he didn't. We all would have heard if he ended something like that."

"You seem to care a little more when I call it by its real name. You don't hate it as much. But when I call it Obamacare, yeah I get that reaction on your face right now."

"Never knew that was its name but regardless it's not fair to people to force them to have to have medical insurance?"

"We force people to have insurance every day. We can't drive without auto insurance. We can't work without taxes being taken out for roads and infrastructure."

"Motor insurance is necessary to ensure people are protected in cases of accidents. I wouldn't want to have to pay for it. And we all use the roads."

"And health insurance is to ensure people are protected in case of sickness. More people get sick everyday than get into automobile accidents. And without mandatory health insurance we are all paying for the uninsured anyway. Notice the premiums went up after they dropped the individual mandate. Ask yourself why?"

"Tell me why."

"Because now insurance companies are making more money. It's not about the people. Look I don't want to pay taxes but I do. You remember the first check you got when you saw how much was taken out for taxes. You didn't even want to work no more after that."

Both laugh

"I sure didn't. That was definitely a wakeup call."

More laughter

"I'm just playing devil's advocate here I see both sides of the health care issue but I think it's done way more help than its done harm. Health care costs are out of control."

"That they are. And this was before Obamacare I'll give you that. Fifty dollars for an aspirin. I'd have to be almost dying to go to the hospital and I could afford it."

"So here's my problem with Trump. He don't give a fuck. He don't give a fuck about you, me, nobody. He don't give a fuck about his own wife. Look at the way he treats her, like property."

"He's grabbed her by the pussy I'm sure."

Laughs

"You said that not me."

Laughs

"You know one of his first acts as President was to allow coal companies to dump toxic chemicals into streams, into waterways. I know it's a little more complicated than that but that is what he allowed. How is it that companies are allowed to dump anything into our waterways? At the end of the day, just as you wished because when you were voting you only thought about you, which I understand, but what Trump did was allow companies to get their way and said a big F U to people and the environment just like he said if you listened hard enough. Excuse my language but he's shitting on the people who voted for him. He's pulling services for our elderly, for the shut-in. Things that across the demographics lower income people need. He cut the budget to Meals on Wheels. If you aren't rich he isn't for you and doesn't care about you. The agency that protects financial lenders from charging minorities more than white people, they no longer enforce this protection. Tips. He made it law that businesses can keep the tips restaurant patrons give to their waiters and waitresses. So now your favorite restaurant can keep your waiters tip. Then when the Labor Department learned it would cost workers 5.8 billion dollars Trump's administration buried the data."

"Don't you think Hillary would have done the same thing? Shitted on the people who got her elected. You already said you had concerns."

"That's a good question. A very good question. I don't think she would have taken this country as far down the wrong path Trump has. I don't think she would have sold us out so blatantly for the rich but we will never know. But that's also why I voted for Bernie."

"What do you mean by taken us down this path? What wrong path has Trump taken us down?"

"He says he wants to make America great again. First that implies that America isn't great anymore."

"It's just a slogan."

"Slogans are words and words misused are dangerous. Can we be honest and say that's nothing but a racist way of saying he wants to make America white again. Especially after the fact the last president was black. Trump still questions Obama's birth certificate and he's out of office. Trump's first pardon was of a sheriff who was convicted of abusing his power against, wait let me see, brown people, oh and he's another birther conspiracy guy."

"No I can't say that. He may see only green but he's not a racist and his slogan had nothing to do with Obama. And he agreed publicly his birth certificate was fine and that Obama was an American citizen. Now the sheriff thing. That was sketchy but all presidents have some sketchy pardons on their record. Presidents and governors alike."

"Publicly he may have stated that, but read what the people around him have said he says privately."

"You can't believe leaks from anonymous sources."

"When the leaks are well sourced and coming from the White House. Anyway he's made a laughing stock of this great nation. Do you think our reputation around the globe is better than it was before he was elected?"

"Our reputation hasn't taken a hit. This is still the best and most dominant country in the world."

"You've seen his tweets. This guy is a political moron. He retweeted a racist conspiracy theory, one proven false by the way, that drew a rebuke from England and their Parliament. Our biggest ally. Why do you think he hasn't visited the UK? Because he's not welcome. They have their own racism problem they don't need the supposed to be leader of the free world exacerbating it. He couldn't even go open a US embassy. One he blamed on President Obama when the process was started by President Bush. Then his apology was 'if you want to apologize I will apologize', to a reporter. He never even apologized because he knew what he was doing. He retweeted what an ideology he believes. And this nonsense with North Korea."

"Wait, his threat of fire and brimstone kept North Korea from doing something stupid."

"You can't scare crazy men from doing something stupid. He's poking the bear ready to ignite a nuclear war trying to show how tough he is."

"He's trying to stop a nuclear war from happening. Sometimes you have to show the bully you're not going to be bullied. Sometimes you have to pump up your chest. Sometimes it's only down the barrel of a gun you can get the enemy to stand down."

"And do you know how that almost always ends. In a fight. But this time these two have nuclear weapons, not fists or even guns. You pull a gun on someone they don't forget it. They may stand down in the moment but it is never over right there. They always come back."

"But even South Korea said Trump brought North Korea back to the table."

"He could have done that privately too without scaring the world into thinking a New Cold War is brewing. And how much of that from North Korea was really about getting their athletes into the Olympics? Are they really at the table. Are they really stopping their nuclear program? I thought not."

"Is there anything you like about him?"

"No. I don't like a racist who puts the whole world in danger. This aint no game show."

"You have to be open minded. There has to be something you approve of he's done."

"There is. I think he's ripped off this fake façade we've been living behind and forced the country to deal with issues which needed to be addressed. He's shown the faces of racism, misogyny, and more dangerous, elitism are still real. People need to talk about them and be honest about the problems like you and I are here doing. G.I. Joe taught me as a kid"

"Knowing is half the battle."

"Exactly. Knowing is half the battle. Knowledge is the key. But for as much as we've been talking racial issues the bigger problem is monetary issues. The fact that most of the world's wealth is held by a minuscule number of people, the 1%. The 1% that 80 plus percent of Trump's tax breaks go to. Financial inequality is a bigger problem than racial inequality the world over. Even though I think he's the Devil's Proxy I think he has forced people to deal with some uncomfortable topics. I think, I hope in the long run we as a nation will be better for it, for facing the dragon hiding under our beds."

"I think we can agree there. Even though I don't think it is as much of a problem as you do I think we can agree there's work that can be done."

"So how is that you're defending this guy? He's a piece of shit human being. A fact that white people and even some black people overlooked or didn't understand when they voted for him."

"Why does he have to be a piece of shit human being? What gives you the right to call him that?"

"I only call it how I see it. Remember he just grabs them by the pussy. Look at all the women accusing him of sexual misconduct. If he wasn't the president and being protected by those who wave money at him, since that's all he seems to love, and use him as a puppet he might not even be able to run his own company with those allegations. Many men have been taken down by less than what he's accused of. Also look at his immigration policy. He only wants white people coming into the country. Not people from shithole Africa or Haiti. You know Haiti, the country where everybody has AIDS. But those from Norway he wants them. And the neo-nazis and klansman in Charlottesville, they're good people. Get out of there with his nonsense. But more specifically let's look at his record. It's more than just color. Can you name me one thing he has done do help any American who isn't rich? Just one. One thing."

Silent Pause.

"Quiet right because you can't."

"What did President Obama do in his eight years in office?"

"First let's start with Bin Laden. That was his call."

"Bin Laden and health care which is a disaster. What else has he done? What has he done to help anyone who isn't rich as per your criteria?"

"Well there's the climate change agreement he signed with every other industrialized nation of the world that this president dropped out of drawing scorn from around the world if I may remind you. There's his turnaround of the economy which was in a recession when President Obama took office. You're military, he repealed Don't Ask Don't Tell allowing our countrymen and women to serve freely. Do you have a problem with LGBQT, excuse me if I have the letters mixed up, but do you have a problem with serving alongside them?"

"I know some soldiers who did but not me. I don't care who you sleep with at night. As long as you're not trying to hit on me 'cause I don't swing that way, when it comes to service for this country I believe anyone should be eligible. That's between you, the other person and God. I may have a problem with homosexuality but not when it comes to service to our country. Whether you believe in God or not. As long as when the shit hit the fan you've got my back, as long as you can follow orders and help the person next to you come home safely I could care less about your sex life as long as your not trying to hit on me. And if it keeps people from being drafted, if it keeps my son from being drafted. Yeah, I'm ok with it. At the end of the day they are people first. If you can point and shoot and defend I'm all for you."

"So what else did President Obama do? There's the Dreamers, Net Neutrality, and of particular importance to black people he changed the culture at the Department of Justice. He tried to bring it to a place of fair and equal punishment. He actually started holding white people responsible for their crimes. And now that I'm thinking about it I, besides all the myriads of reasons, Obama passed reform cracking down on those scam profit colleges like Trump University. And I could go on and on about what President Obama accomplished and you can't name one thing other than tax reform the guy in office now has. Tax reform which by the way helps the rich and no one else. And President Obama, he actually loves his wife, showed every person what it is to live with class and dignity and not grab women by the pussy. And cheat on her with porn stars. You want to talk about Monica Lewinsky what about Stormy Daniels and the $130,000 he paid for her silence."

"That's your go-to line to diss Trump, he was joking."

"He said it. And he meant it and you know it."

"He didn't mean it and if he did, there's nothing that can be done about it now. If you don't like him put up with him until re-election time comes. The man definitely has his flaws but he was the best option."

"Is that what you said about Obama or were you one of the he's not my President."

"I know those types as I'm sure you do but me personally he had the job so I said let him do his job."

"And a great job he did."

"But like you said with Clinton. In my mind Trump was and still is the better of two evils. If she can't protect a US consulate after they told her what was coming then how can I trust her. After they knew they needed help and asked for it then how could I think she could keep the country safe. As a soldier it wasn't something I could accept. At the end of the day with this guy in office I believe I have a greater chance of staying secure than with her. So yeah I can ignore all the other stuff to keep me safe."

"From the same guy who wants to start a nuclear war over Twitter with North Korea. I see your line of thinking and I understand your safety concerns but this guy has some screws loose. And even with Hillary in office do you think the United States military and law enforcement officers couldn't keep the country safe?"

"I'm sure they could have but leadership starts from the top. And what would you have done about North Korea then since you know everything?"

"I definitely don't know everything, maybe a lot but not everything. What I do know is, what did Roosevelt say, walk softly and carry a big stick. We have the biggest baddest stick on the planet. You and your teammates when you served. My cousins and theirs now. You don't need to publicly flaunt it to prove they are there. If you're a cop I don't need to see the gun to know you have one. It's like the crazy guy on the block. Everyone is aware he's there. You let him say his peace as he screams at no one in particular, you know he's crazy. But you keep an eye on him. You tell your kids don't go nowhere near him. And if he steps out of line then you act. Most crazy people just want to be heard, they want their rant to be heard. You give them a forum and then the rant progresses to the next level. The crazy guy in the house. He just yells from the porch. He'll never step off the porch though unless you acknowledge him. He may be crazy but he knows better. It didn't need a response. I'm sorry. It didn't' need a public response. There's no need to poke crazy people publicly."

"And that dude is insane."

"Money is the root of all evil but unbridled power is the loss of all sanity."

"Amen to that, I like that saying but all I'm saying is his tactic worked."

"We'll see. And one more. Obama, even though he should have just made marijuana legal he all but decriminalized it allowing states to figure out what they wanted to do with it. Now the racist Attorney General. Wait before I continue can you agree the Attorney General of the United States is racist?"

"No I can't. Everybody can't be a racist. He may be stuck in the past but every white person in a position of power isn't a racist."

"I never said they were. But if he talks like a racist, if his actions are racist, then a racist he must be."

"He never would have been confirmed for the position if Congress would have found him to be racist. If there was any evidence. And other than a thirty year old letter from Coretta Scott King there is no proof of what you're accusing him of being."

"Wow. I'm happy you know her name and didn't call her the wife of Reverend Dr. King."

"Now who's being racist?"

"I'm not trying to be. A smart ass maybe but I'm actually ecstatic. Especially from someone who never learned a lick of black history until life taught him in the military. But continue. I apologize for cutting you off."

"No I was done. You're going to call a man racist yet you have no proof."

"Of course I don't know the man but he has opposed every immigration bill since he's been in the Senate."

"That only proves he doesn't like immigration, not that he's a racist."

"And he's only opposed immigration of brown and black people. We never have any discussions about immigration from Scotland or Belgium or any other predominantly white country, not Germany or imagine if we didn't let Italians into the country or the Polish or the Irish. Beside the letter from Mrs. King, his own colleagues testified, put their hand on the Bible and testified he used the n-word and looked fondly on the klu klux klan."

"That would make him racist if it were true but how do we know that wasn't just political drama?"

"But you're ignoring my question about the predominantly white countries. Why is there never any talk on limiting immigration form those countries?"

"Maybe because people from those countries immigrate legally and none of that has anything to do with the Jeff Sessions."

"We'll have to agree to disagree on him. But back to the point. Obama, to the want and desire of the individual states and the majority of the country as a whole decriminalized marijuana use. Let them tax it. Or more precisely had the federal government look the other way and allowed the states to determine how to control the access to marijuana in its borders and now this guy reverses it. Even congress, both sides have decried this action."

"That's the law. Right now marijuana is illegal. He's just enforcing the law."

"But he picks and chooses what laws and crimes to go after as the country's top cop. Isn't there a better use for federal resources then going after something no one cares about? Something the states that have allowed and have used to add to its resources. It's added so much money to the coffers of those states and now he did what he did."

"But it is illegal. And most marijuana is brought into the country illegally by gangs and cartels."

"Another reason why you should legalize it. Let the states handle it and profit from it cutting off the need of distribution form the gangs and cartels."

"How do we even know marijuana is safe?"

"Which is more dangerous, marijuana or alcohol?"

"They both are dangerous."

"So why is alcohol legal and marijuana not?"

"Because alcohol is not a gateway drug."

"See here's the thing about statistics like you said earlier and I agree with. I had a professor tell me that if you want to prove something, anything, you can find a statistic to prove your point. 90% of drug users started with weed. But 90% of weed users never matriculate to another drug. And plus just real life I've never seen marijuana kill someone's liver. And on top of that how many people are killed by drunk drivers every year, everyday? People who smoke just want to relax. They're not out there getting drunk trying to fight. Now I'm not saying make alcohol illegal but what I am saying is alcohol is legal because its left up to adults to handle responsibly. Adults should have the same responsibility with weed. If they want it let them have it just put certain restrictions in place. The same as alcohol."

"You are a very logical thinker you know that."

"I've been called worse. And with my logical mind I can't explain how you overlook white supremacy, racism, bigotry, misogyny, sexism, elitism, and"

"And grabbing them by the pussy?"

"I wasn't going there, I was going to say and a President's uncontrollable appetite to crush anyone, including the media and Congress, anyone who questions him. He doesn't want to make America great again. He wants to divide and conquer. Simple and plain. But enough about him what do you think about term limits for Congress?"

"I'm against it. Why kick a man or woman out of office because of some arbitrary timeline? If the people of a state want the person removed they will vote the person out."

"Not true?"

"What do you mean it's not true?"

"It's not. Something like 90% of incumbent Congressman and women get reelected."

"Then that means they are doing their job."

"But Congress has around a 10% approval rating."

"Maybe overall but what's the approval rating in their home town and home state. Congress doesn't answer to everyone they answer to the constituents of their state."

"I bet you it's not good. How is it the President of the United States and most though not all state governors and city mayors have term limits but not Congress?"

"The President has term limits because it is the most powerful position in the world. That's too much power for one man to hold for that long."

"And Congress is equal to the President in power."

"But its split up amongst all of the Senators and State Representatives. It's not one person wielding all the power."

"Yet the people, even though they vote, don't really have a vote always."

"You're crazy."

"No I'm serious. If you're from a Republican state, your incumbent Republican senator will almost always win reelection. Why? Because people vote for party. Nine out of ten people don't cross that line."

"More like nine hundred and ninety nine out of a thousand but yeah you're right."

"So if you're a democrat in a republican state running for Congress, unless the incumbent fucks up somehow he or she is getting reelected. The Republicans aren't going to put a strong candidate against the incumbent. It just doesn't happen, on either side. So the incumbent gets the Republican nod and because it's a republican state they get reelected."

"So you want to institute term limits because the voting public is lazy?"

"Sometimes you have to protect people from themselves. Like coaches trying to stop a concussed football player from going back in the game. Or Congress not allowing Roosevelt to become too powerful and instituting term limits on the office of the President."

"I can't agree with that. Let people decide who represents them."

"That's the thing. People don't. Republicans vote republican and democrats vote democrat. Unless there is a state with a close count of the two the incumbent will win. And once they are in then they do crazy things like redraw voting districts to ensure they stay in. And come up with all these voter laws."

"We need voter laws. It's the only way to ensure people aren't rigging the vote."

"Do you just regurgitate everything you read? All these new voter laws are designed to do is to stop the poor from voting. That's it. And pay attention because this is only Republican states trying to do this."

"To surpass the black vote?"

"To suppress the vote of a group of people who won't in large numbers won't vote Republican."

"You really believe all these conspiracy theories don't you. These laws are to stop voter fraud."

"Open your eyes. I don't believe in conspiracies at all. I don't believe what anybody tells me either. Question everything and learn. When you leave here look into it. Read up on the truth. And from multiple sources."

"Do you believe in the Illuminati?"

"If you're asking is there some super-secret super-elite group of individuals plotting the next move of society for their own financial gain, moving people around the chess board of life like pawns, some group who wields power from the shadows I don't know." Laugh. "I guess it's possible. Anything is possible when a group of determined people put their brains and resources to it. But the reality of it is I'm not one of them. I have to focus on my day to day life. I have kids to raise and a family to feed. Conspiracy theories are great, they may be true they may not be. We might have landed on the moon we might not have. Personally I don't care. It doesn't affect me on a day-to-day basis. It's not something I'm worried about. But since we're on this line of thought, wait, first why do you ask, do you know something, are they hiding the existence of aliens from us?"

"No. I don't know anything. I'm just trying to get a complete picture of the person in front of me."

"You'll never get that. Not in one sitting. Not in one day. Not in one year. I'm too complex." Laughs. "So what about aliens, do you believe in them?"

"This is the way I look at aliens. Whether you believe in God or whether you believe in the theory of evolution I don't know how you don't believe in aliens. I think it's a human frailty to think we are the only people in the entire vast universe. If you believe in God and the Bible, all the Bible says is God created the Heavens and the Earth. Then it speaks on what God did here on earth. There is no mention of what He did or didn't do elsewhere. What He might have done after He created the earth or before. Now on the other hand if you believe in the theory of evolution how is it that out of all the planets out there in the universe, the millions of planets, that this one was the only planet where creatures evolve and now we have humans? Isn't it scientifically possible that if humans evolved to live on Earth's geography and live in Earth's atmosphere that other living creatures, aliens would evolve to live on their planet's geography and in their atmosphere? In the millions of trillions of planets you're telling me life only exists on one planet. Nah I don't believe that so yes I believe in aliens. Now I'm not saying they've visited the earth or that they haven't visited the earth because I really don't know. I'm not saying they're out there taking people from their homes and doing experiments on them but I can't not believe they don't exist. But what I do know for certain is that if aliens did visit that the Earth and if one did crash land in Roswell that the U.S. government is more than capable of covering it up and plotting with or coercing or all out forcing other countries to do the same."

"Your logic makes sense I'll give you that but until I see one I'll never be convinced."

"You believe you breathe oxygen though you've never seen it. You believe in God whom you've never seen."

"I can't see oxygen but I can at least see my breath especially on a cold day. And God created all so I have faith. But aliens are just too far-fetched. And do you have any belief in the institution of law. You seem to believe anybody with power is against you."

"Where did that come from? I believe in law but power, power is another thing. And power can be and is abused on a daily basis."

"The more powerful rule or fear get conquered."

"So is this why you think the government is covering up aliens, because they can. Because they have the power."

"You're not listening to what I'm saying. I didn't say they would or that they did, I said they are capable of covering it up especially if they thought it was in the best nature of safety. And yes they have the power. Even Spiderman taught us with great power comes great responsibility so don't for a second think if they thought it was the right thing to do they wouldn't shield us from the truth."

"So you're going all X-Files on me now?"

"Don't think this government won't do those things it accuses others of doing. We have an atom bomb, nuclear bombs, but we don't want other countries to have them. They are too dangerous for them we'll say and they are but maybe because they're too dangerous for us too. But people need security so you can go back and forth with that debate."

"Like Area 51?"

"Exactly. Area 51, which up until what a decade ago the government didn't even acknowledge. It wasn't until other satellites proved its existence."

"Even though residents of Nevada knew not to go near or it they would disappear."

"Our government wouldn't do stuff like that. They wouldn't make American citizens disappear."

"You're kidding me right. Have you ever heard of The Tuskegee Experiment? They didn't make these people disappear but they sure experimented on them. And just so you know wasn't the only experiment our government has conducted in the name of science or security or both on people. You do know that right?"

"What's the Tuskegee Experiment?"

"Really, you've never heard of the Tuskegee Experiment. Do you know who Emmett Till is?"

"No. Is he a rapper?"

"See this is the other problem. In your schools outside of Martian Luther King and now maybe Barack Obama were you ever taught anything about black history?"

"I went to a school of all white students in a little town in the south. Do you really think we were taught Black History? We were taught American history. What black history I've learned came out of curiosity and google."

"And how many black people did you learn about in school because I learned about a whole ton of white people through all the years of American history classes? Have you ever learned about any black people who were instrumental to American History?"

"Not much to be honest."

"How is it that you're only taught the Anglo-Saxon view of the growth of America? Did they even call slavery slavery when you were being taught?"

"Yes, but unfortunately when my youngest child was taught they used a different word, they tried to sanitize it."

"Was he or she taught more than just white American history in school?"

"I don't know. I never really asked."

"And you wonder why you have a prejudice, even if subtle, why you have a prejudice and fear of black people even if before today you didn't think you did. Because we as humans fear the unknown. And you have a need for security. Now let me explain to you what The Tuskegee Experiment was and why I say never put anything past the government. Even those things you think the government wouldn't go so far to do. The Tuskegee Experiment was a government led science project. They gathered a bunch of poor black people and experimented on them with syphilis. You know what syphilis is?"

"Yeah I know what syphilis is."

"Now some of these people had the disease before the project started but the rest who didn't were given the disease. Let's start there, the American government purposefully gave a disease to a group of poor black people. A debilitating disease they knew the effects of."

"Wait. So did these people know what they were getting themselves into? They voluntarily agreed to this for some kind of payment I'm assuming."

"No they didn't. The men who had it before the experiment started were never told they had it and the people they gave it to never knew. They were told they were getting free health care not being given a disease. Then the government tracked how they lived with it. Even after penicillin was known to be a cure for syphilis they didn't cure these people."

"Wow never knew that. I can't excuse a program like that but how long ago did this happen? Those kind of things would never happen now."

"It started in the 1930's and ran through the seventies. And there have been other 'research' done on countless drugs and their effect on people as well as radiation tests on live human beings, Americans. All in the name of science. So if you have a government who will do that to its own people, even though you think we've progressed and things like this aren't happening anymore, what else are they doing we don't know about? You already believe they might be covering up the existence of aliens if it suited their purpose? If they thought it was in the best interest of the world? Man I know you're busy living your life and running your business. And that's great I'm not knocking it but there is more going on in the world than what's going on in your life. And until you understand those things you'll be ignorant when you comment on something, like what led us to this conversation in the first place."

"Some things are ignorance. I don't speak on those things. Some things are a matter of opinion. I will speak on those things if I choose to do so. Like you I will not be silenced because someone said shut up. It doesn't work that way. I don't work that way. I'd rather be quiet on a subject then run with it as far as you take things like government conspiracies."

"That's good because I would never ask you to be silent. I would suggest anyone become informed before they speak on a topic but I would never ask anyone to shut up because two things happen when you speak."

"And again I didn't say they covered up anything, what I said was they are capable of doing it. There's a difference. And what are the two things that happen when we speak?"

"You either show your knowledge on a subject or you show your ignorance which comes off as stupidity for speaking on something you know nothing about."

"Can we talk about the police?"

"Of course we can. I've been waiting for this topic too."

"Do you have a problem with the police and policing in general?"

"Let me start by asking you this. Did your father have to have a conversation with you about how to deal with police if you get stopped or pulled over, even if you didn't do anything wrong?"

"No. Why should he. It's common sense. You do what you're asked and you go home."

"That's your reality. I understand that. But that's not our reality. I know I'm about to get really deep here but just go with me. As a white man you don't have to worry about if you got stopped by a racist cop. If you got stopped and this cop was going to give you unlawful orders because he believed just because of the color of your skin you either were a drug dealer, a drug user, or an illegal alien. And most of all you never have to worry about going home alive. Let's start there."

"Most cops aren't like that. Maybe one out of a million."

"But the thing is you don't have to worry about that one out of a million. You're thing is safety form what I've gathered so far."

"Yes, safety is high up on my list."

"Well your interactions with an officer as a lawful citizen, you don't have to worry about what might happen. I do. My son does. It's the way it is. Do you know there are still places where if you drive south down I-95 where black people warn other black people not to stop. And west towards the idwest away from major cities. If you want gas get it on the highway stations they'll tell you. Don't get off the highway and definitely don't pull over in these little towns. And it's not just because of the people, it's more because of the police."

"That's just fear. A fear you have to get over. That stuff doesn't exist anymore. I mean it may exist in a few places across the country but it's not prevalent anymore."

"I was going to a small rural town on business and I had a state trooper friend, a white guy, he told me 'You don't want to stop there especially after dark. Stay on the highway and do not speed' is what he said so don't tell me it's not prevalent anymore. This is a state trooper in 2018 telling me this. But you know what's worse. What's worse is I understand why. Let me explain it to you. That same fear you have if you saw a group of young black males in the mall. That fear comes from ignorance. Not the societal definition of ignorance as dumb I mean the dictionary definition of ignorance as not knowing. Again we fear the unknown. So you take that fear, because cops are people to, take that fear and add the stereotype of blacks being gang bangers and drug dealers, and the fact that every cop wants two things. One and the most important thing all cops want is to be able go home after their shift to their family every day. Two is to move up through the ranks. How do you move up you make arrests. Prove you're a good cop. How do you go home every night, you're always aware for trouble lurking around the corner. Have your cop antenna up. Now if you already believe in the stereotype of black people then every time you see one your antenna starts going off, of course unless it's someone you know is not a threat. Am I losing you here?"

"No. Go on. I'm listening."

"Now if you're a cop and you pull over a suburban white woman who you deem not a threat there's almost nothing she can do to make the situation go bad outside of putting her hand on the police. But if you're a nineteen year old black male who fits the stereotype of a threat the officer's guard is already pre-raised, his gun is pulled because he or she wants to go home safe. Now any move this nineteen year old kid makes could cause him to lose his life because the cop looked at him as a threat, a threat to their safety, a threat to them going home. Now that kid who only remembered oh my insurance card is not in the glove compartment it's in the arm rest lost his life because he did something he didn't understand was going to get him killed. He thought he was complying with the officer's instructions to get the insurance card and registration not knowing his move from the glove compartment to the armrest was alarming for this cop. This cop started out scared going in and it cost a kid his life. Now here's the interesting to part to all of this. Too many times black people have lost their lives because of scared cops who had no need to be scared. A man sitting inside his car with his arms raised. A man running away. A man standing on the highway next to a broken down car. A car full of kids driving away. In each of these instances someone lost their life because a cop was scared for no other reason than the person was black and the preconceived notion that cop brought to the scene with them. But it's not always just black people. It's just with black people most often the cop had the stereotype of fear before the incident started. There are other times like the hotel video where there was no preconceived bias or prejudice the cop just got scared and shot. Or when a store clerk calls in and says there is a suspicious man. Oh but the suspicious man is always black bad example."

"Could it be that police, let me ask it this way. In your city. If a cop works in a drug infested neighborhood. A neighborhood let's say that's predominantly black."

"Ok but before you continue on know that even in my city there are drug infested neighborhoods of mostly black people yes. But there are drug infested neighborhoods of mostly white people also. And some of mostly other ethnicities. Stop believing drugs are only a problem in the black community. And I live in the suburbs now. Moved out there so my daughter could have a better education without it costing me fifty thousand dollars a year. And out there in the suburbs is a high school the kids call heroin high. Now this high school is in a very affluent neighborhood with kids driving very expensive cars to school. So drugs and drug use in not a black people problem. The better neighborhoods just hide the drugs better but they're still drug infested. When I was young I went to the best high school in the city and I could find drugs whenever I wanted if I wanted so it's not only black communities where drugs are a problem. The money in some places just masks it where other neighborhoods, the poverty can't hide the drugs. But continue on."

"Understood. But my example is if I'm a cop and all the people I keep arresting are black people wouldn't that lead me to be more cautious around black people."

"If you're an officer of the law and you think that you shouldn't be a cop. Because even in the poorest neighborhoods the majority of people living there are law abiding citizens. If you're a cop and your district is a black neighborhood then of course you'll be arresting black people. You come from a small town of majority white people. So if there are crimes being committed there who is committing them? It would have to be white people am I right?"

"Yes but in a small town everyone knows everyone so the anonymity goes out the window. They know who to be afraid of."

"But that's a small town. In a big city they don't know everyone. Or if it's a small town and an outsider comes through are they going to be scared because they don't know anything about this person. If that same small town white city cop left and went on vacation he's not going to be afraid of white people because all he's seen is white people committing crimes is he?"

"Cops are like soldiers, when they go on vacation they are still cops, that is in their blood but they're not on duty. They're not actively looking for crime. It's not really the people but the neighborhood."

"And the people in the neighborhood?"

"What about them. What complicity do they have? They know what's going on but y'all have this no snitching thing."

"No, we don't have this no snitching thing. We have this look out for your own health kind of thing. For your own safety kind of thing. You know the safety thing that got you to vote for Trump. The safety thing that got you to ignore his other more nefarious traits. You see the police in these neighborhoods can't protect people from everything. Yeah they are only a phone call away but who protects them after the police leave and before they get there once you make that 9-1-1 call. That's why people don't tell. They're afraid."

"So you agree with this no snitching nonsense?"

"No, I don't. But I understand. You can't say what you would do if you were in that situation."

"But it's mostly criminals."

"That's a stupid ass question and a stupid ass statement. Most people even in poor neighborhoods aren't criminals one. And two do you really expect criminals to snitch. Let's be real here. They aint saying a word until they get caught. Then they'll start signing like Beyoncé."

"I'd do whatever it takes to get out that situation. I did whatever it took to get out of that situation. First the military then I went back to school."

"Good for you. But everybody aint you. And if you needed to again I have no doubt you would do whatever it took again. Let's say if your business failed and I'm not wishing any ill will to your business. But you can't knock those who don't. Some don't know how to. Some tried and didn't make it. Everyone has a reason and a story."

"So why does your community hate black cops?"

"Cops, inside their buildings they have their own fight as any and all black people do in any job. But outside, on the streets they're like the military. It's them against the world. Once they put on that uniform they are no longer black, or white, or brown, they're blue."

"So you're saying there shouldn't be black cops."

"I'm definitely not saying anything like that. The idea of not having black policemen is idiotic. Every community needs to be represented when it comes to policing. Just imagine how bad it would be if there were no black cops. You can't, I can't but plenty of people can remember what it was like before. Anybody who says black cops are traitors and stuff like that, they are idiots. We need them there fighting for us, for our rights from the inside. We all just wish they would fight more but everybody is not built for every fight. They could be in there protecting us but we would never find that out so saying we don't need them is dead wrong. But not just black cops, all cops. Now when one of your own is wrong we need you to stand up and say they were wrong. Look at old Dr. King videos. There were a lot of white people out there protesting and marching with them. Like Bernie Sanders. Today though, that doesn't happen enough."

"So you have a problem with the police?"

"Why are you trying to get me to say I have a problem with the police. I do not. 99.99% of the time at least I don't. But that .01%, this is my issue with the police. And the crazy part is like I said I understand why to a certain extent. Take this. If you put a very large group of any single category of people, however you choose to categorize them there is going to be a bad apple in the group. And when I say large I mean thousands plus. No matter how you categorize them, a large group of men, women, white people, black people, protestors, Asians, those over twenty, juveniles, construction workers, architects, bus drivers, soldiers, fisherman, whoever, no matter what the category if the group is big enough statically speaking there is going to be some bad individuals in the group. Now 99.99% of the group will be great upstanding individuals. But that .01% will still be bad. So that means in a group of say a hundred thousand people, .01% is ten individuals who are bad people. My problem with the police is they protect that .01% those 10 cops. And they make excuses for them, Viceroy Sarah Sanders Kelly Conway style."

"You had to get that jab in."

"I did. But the police, they know who the bad cops are amongst their ranks but they do little to remove them. Talk to them if you know any, they'll tell you. Then when something unthinkable happens their leadership, they Trump us. They lie to our face. They give us these alternative facts. Nowadays it's easy to know when the police are lying if there is video of the incident. When the video exonerates the officer they can't wait to show it. It's on every news channel. When the video is damaging they do whatever it takes not to show it or they show it and tell you to your face it's okay, it's not a chokehold or its ok the person made a move and the go-to, the officer thought he might have had a gun and feared for his life. How is that ok? How is it that cops have cameras that they can turn on and off? How is it that video is not public record? How is it that city and state governments are passing laws making police body cam footage unavailable to the public? These are the things that make people not trusting of the cops. The decision their leadership makes to protect the guilty amongst their ranks builds on that tension making it worse. And like I said earlier it's not all cops. And I feel sorry to a certain extent for the police."

"Why?"

"Because now they fell what it's like to be black."

"Huh?"

"Now the police know what it's like to be stereotyped. You see black people have been stereotyped by the police for so long because of the actions of a few within their community. Now cops are being stereotyped by the actions of the minority within their community. Now they have to work with a stigma my community has had to my whole life. When the actions of the .01% define the actions of the 99.99%. No it's not fair. But it wasn't fair when it was being applied to black people, and it hasn't changed much, but it was never fair to black people and it's not fair to the police but it is what it is. Now answer me this, when is a choke hold not a choke hold?"

"When it's on tape being administered by the police in New York."

"You ever been to New York?"

"Many times."

"Me too. I love the city."

"But what about the NYPD, you have a problem with them?"

"I have no problem with the NYPD or any police agency. You keep asking that question. I love the police. Grown people love the police. I need someone to call. But that doesn't mean I can't tell them when they're wrong. I tell my kids when they're wrong. Coaches tell their players when they're wrong. Citizens should be able to tell the police when they are wrong without being called traitors or cop haters. Just like I wouldn't say one stick up kid with a mask who happens to be black was a representative of the whole race of black people I wouldn't say one bad decision by one bad cop was a representation of the whole department. Like I wouldn't say one serial killer who was white was a representation of all white people."

"But that one cop needed to go instead of being defended, like the serial killer and the robber would have been jailed."

"Ah, now you're getting it."

"But why should one man lose his job for a mistake, especially one he might have been trained to do."

"Because a man lost his life. When you go to court they don't care if it is your first offense when they judge you, you're either guilty or you're not guilty."

"But when they go to sentence you the judge will take that into account. There's different punishments for murder. The sentence for premeditated murder isn't the same as involuntary as involuntary murder."

"But you get punished you don't walk free. Even involuntary murder comes with jail time. It's no slap on the wrist."

"You're right about that."

"We need to hold the police to the same standard we hold everyday people."

"But if I accidentally run somebody over I'm not going to jail, provided I wasn't drunk or something like that."

"But if I accidentally shot you I'm going to jail. People have gone to jail for accidentally shooting themselves. If you accidentally run me over more than likely I ran out in front of you and you couldn't stop in time. It wasn't your fault. But you have to choose to shoot someone. Pulling a trigger is a choice. And if it is a choice made out of fear maybe you're in the wrong profession."

"That's why academics don't make good soldiers."

"That's why cops who don't know the streets don't make good cops. Passing a test on a computer is one thing. Being able to control your body and emotions in a highly tense situation is another."

"Interesting way to phrase it."

"You have no opinion of the police?"

"Like you said my interaction with the police is different. I don't live in fear of any interaction and up until you explained it I didn't understand why anyone would. I guess I'm lucky I don't have to worry about whether I'm here or there or what they might think of me."

"You mean you don't worry about being pulled over and having the police take your money because they suspect you of drug dealing. You probably think they'd need proof."

"Of course they'd need proof. You are innocent until proven guilty in this country."

"Not in every case. You would think they would but they don't always need any proof. They can seize your money on the 'belief' you're doing something illegal, it's called highway interdiction. Its why I don't drive around with any major amounts of cash."

"Why would you?"

"It shouldn't matter why if you have no proof of a crime committed? How is that not illegal seizure?"

"I'm not in law enforcement but I'm sure they have some regulations they have to follow."

"I also want you to look this up. The majority of these seizures happen in areas where the majority of the population are white but the majority of the people being stopped and having their money taken are out of state and not white but let's change the subject."

"No wait don't change the subject. How many of those stops, where the money was taken, how many of those were legit stops where the people were actually criminals?"

"I don't know. But too many, with one being too many, too many were unjustified and had money taken from innocent people who then have no recourse to getting their money back. Something's not right there. But like I said let's move on. There's something I want to ask you. As a white man what do you think of the black lives matters movement?"

"I think its bullshit."

"Okay you really meant that."

"I did. All lives matter. I not saying black people don't matter. I'm not saying black people are being treated equally or fairly in all circumstances. I'm not even saying we don't have a long way to go as a nation when it comes to race relations and the treatment of black people and all people of color and even women. And I will say I've learned a lot today. But what I'm also am saying is black lives matters is divisive. Yes, your life matters. But so does mine. So does my neighbor's down the street. So does every person in this wonderful country of ours. Now like I said I'm not saying we are there, I'm not saying things are perfect. I'm just saying black lives aren't the only lives that matter. And if black lives really mattered so much to those people then what are they really doing about it except blocking traffic and protesting. What tangible results are they creating? What positive things have they done? Even Colin Kaepernick, I don't respect what he did, not standing but at least he put his money where his mouth was. I can respect the action he took. He actually saw what he saw as a problem and did something about it. I may not respect his method of protest but I respect his actions. These black live matters people all they do is nothing. As a black man what do you think about black lives matter?"

"I think the movement brought attention to a problem. It brought attention to the plight of black people dealing with the police. No matter how you want to spin it there is a problem. And I've already expressed to you my issues with the small percentage of the police force. Now this has also been a historical problem. Because let's be honest the police across America, their history when it deals with black people is terrible. And up until the Rodney King video most of white America didn't believe the police did such vile things. All I can say is thank God for cameras and cell phones because now we as a nation are starting to hold the police accountable. Now, except for shining light on the issue, I don't know what black lives matter as an organization have done. I don't even believe, and maybe I'm wrong but I don't even believe that it is a solid coalition of people. It just a group of people voicing their frustration trying to take it from something more than a hashtag. What they're doing now I couldn't tell you."

"So you think black lives matter is good, bad, what? Because I think it has done nothing to move black people forward. All it has done is put a wedge between multiple groups starting with the police, the FOP and any other organization that deals with or supports the police. It was completely unnecessary and counter-productive. Again all lives matter."

"Do you love your child?"

"Yes, what do my children have to do with any of this? And be careful with the next words you speak."

"Relax, I'm not dragging your children into anything. I'm just asking about your love for them."

"I love my kids."

"I'm sure you do. Now if something tragic happened to one of your children, let's say your child was standing on a corner with five other people and a car jumped the curb and your child was the only one hit. Let's say your child was actually the hero. He pushed two of his friends out the way, saved their lives but unfortunately he was hit and hurt badly. While your child is laying on the ground, at that moment what matters to you. You know those other five kids are going to be ok. But it's your child laying on the ground fighting for his life. In that moment when you pray, are you going to pray for your child to survive or are you going to pray for all six kids to survive. In that moment the only thing that matters is your child. Even though I don't follow it, I'm not a member, that's what black lives matter was trying to do. They were trying to put out to the public the fact that black people were being abused by the police. Yes all lives matter but innocent suburban housewives weren't being shot by scared cops."

"Then the execution of the message was terrible because that is not what I got out of it."

"Was the execution of the message bad or did you not want to hear what they had to say? You don't even need to answer that."

"Protests like black lives matters, the NFL protests, protesting the klan when they march. What have they done except turn people off who may have been sympathetic to their cause? Just take the NFL protests. Ok you brought attention to an injustice but the matter in which you did it turned off so many people, people who might have supported it if it was done another way. You can't protest the flag and expect everything to be ok?"

"Was it really a protest against the flag? You know it wasn't."

"It doesn't matter what it really was. That is the way it was perceived which hurt the cause."

"That's the way it was perceived because they didn't want to see it. What you have to realize is for black people no matter what status they reach, no matter how much money they have the stereotype still exists. They still get pulled over. They still get followed in stores. They still get guns pulled on them in situations where guns aren't necessary. These are things they grew up with. These are things that are still happening to their family members. These are things that only don't happen to them when they're recognized. This was a powder keg waiting to blow."

"I understand the reasoning. I do. I sympathize. I just didn't need to see it every Sunday. There are better ways and better places to make their point."

"When? When would it have been a better time? Like you said you didn't want to see it on Sundays. You wouldn't have wanted to see it on Mondays through Fridays because you have a business to run nor Saturday because you want to relax. There is never a good time for something like this. When would these NFL players have had this many eyes on them to make a point? A point that was civil by the way? Not even civil disobedience just a short civil protest. No matter when they did you and everyone else offended wouldn't have wanted to hear it."

"Not true."

"It is true. That's what they said about Tommie Smith and John Carlos too when they raised their fists at the Olympics. Oh that wasn't the time or the place to do it. It's never the time or the place but that's when it actually is the time and the place. In the moment no one wants to admit there is a problem first. Then when would you are forced to take notice you say it's the wrong place for a protest like there ever is a good setting. No matter when they protested you wouldn't have either liked it one or two paid attention unless it was right up in your face. Why? Because it doesn't affect you or the ones you love? Most people, especially people with busy lives, most people don't want to be bothered by the plight of someone else. Why? Because you have your own problems."

"If a group of white players were to protest something before the game they would have been crucified?"

"And the black players weren't? Now you got the wrestling guy, a Trump supporter whose wife was now leads the Small Business Administration for Trump, now he wants to restart his own football league and one of the first things he said was they'll stand for the flag. FYI he's nobody's master. He may be some people's boss but he's nobody's master. Like some refused to watch NFL over the protests I'll never watch a minute of the XFL because of what he said. How he presented it. They'll get not one penny from me."

"So you don't watch wrestling?"

"Not anymore."

"I can respect that. I like your conviction. But back to the NFL. They did nothing to the players protesting. If this was a group of white players leading a protest it would have been silenced."

"One that's crazy. In today's social media age nobody gets silenced. It's why the media is always upset. Because now players can go straight to the fans, cut out the middle man. Two what would a group of white players have to protest. Most protests come from inequality? What would white players have to protest about except maybe the number of white players in the league, outside of the quarterback position?"

"At least we still have hockey?"

"I like hockey. But hockey is like soccer in America. It's white for now. It's becoming multi-cultural before our eyes."

"Soccer is changing but hockey won't. Black people don't skate, too cold."

"You may have me there we do prefer islands to igloos."

Laugh

"It's good when we can laugh together."

"It is. And just so you know there are more P.K. Subban's coming."

"I've never served so what is the military actually like? What are the people like? What's it like to serve?"

"The military saved my life so I have nothing bad to say about it. Now don't get me wrong there are assholes in the military too. It's no different than any other walk of life. You get out of it what you put into it. For me it taught me discipline. It taught me focus. I made friends for life in there. Now serving in the military is no different than any other job. You get up, you go to work, you go home. The only difference is you're always at the ready, ready to be deployed, ready to go fight, ready to die because let's face it that's the life of a soldier."

"Is boot camp as bad as they make it seem?"

"Boot camp is designed to weed out the weak. And not weed them like get rid of them. Weed them out like find the weak ones, break them down then build them back up, get them all strong and get the strong ready for war. You know hopefully we never see it but they have to prepare you for the possibility. You know the saying, only the strong survive so the military and boot camp is designed to make you strong even if you thought you were incapable of it. Now don't get me wrong boot camp is hell. Probably the hardest combination of physical and mental exhaustion I've ever had in my life but looking back it helped me get where I am. It took a kid from the south who had no direction in life and gave him direction. For me the military prepared me for life like college does for others straight out of high school. I had guns way before I joined the military but for me the military turned a kid with a gun to a responsible citizen who knew how to handle a gun. Follow me? Do you know what the best part about team sports is?"

"What's that?"

"You ever play any sports growing up?"

"Yeah. Football, basketball, and baseball."

"Then you'll understand what I'm about to say. The best thing about team sports is it teaches you it's not all about you. No matter how good you are you need your teammates to win. You can't score without your teammates. You can't defend against the other team without your teammates. The military is the same way. It teaches you your own importance but at the same it humbles you. You learn real quick it's not all about you. Also, the fact that you get to see the world. It teaches you that in the big view, though you are very important, let's say it teaches you your place in the world. Now the other thing you learn, just like in team sports is that leaders emerge. Everyone can be a soldier, not everyone can lead soldiers. Just like sports, coaches, or in our case some General or maybe even the President, someone not out their putting their life on the line, coaches nor military decision makers aren't on the field of battle putting in the work. They're not taking the shot literally or figuratively. So leaders emerge. It's why some athletes have a hard time leaving their sport. It's the same reason some soldiers can't leave the field. Those military lifers. They don't want to be politicians. They don't want to have to put their soldiers at harm but they will for the greater good. We all understand this. They want to finish their mission. They want the world to be safe and they feel nobody can do what they do. Now I'm not taking anything away from coaches or the pentagon or the Department of Defense or any military decision makers. They have a job to do and they do it exquisitely but at the end of the day they are only calling the plays. Those boots on the ground run them and we run them to perfection."

"You know who Coach Popovich is?"

"Of course I know who Coach Pop is. He is a first ballot Hall of Famer. The coach of the Spurs. Maybe, either him or Red Auerbach, he might be the best coach ever in any sport."

"Yeah him. He passed another coach to rise up the all-time coaching wins list not long ago. Some reporter asked him about it. He said 'I don't remember scoring any points or getting any rebounds'."

"Exactly. Pop is one of the greatest coaches in the NBA. The military could use people like him, people who would be successful anywhere. Any business, organization could have used a Coach Pop. The military has some brilliant people in charge. But he's right, it takes both. No matter how good the hammer you need to know where and when to swing it without hitting yourself in the finger."

"Yeah that hurts."

"Yeah it does. And out there it doesn't just hurt you. It's hurts your family, your friends, your loved ones, your whole community when someone doesn't come home. Every time someone dies the country hears about it, no matter how numb we've become, it still hurts."

"Each and every time. So you loved your time in the military?"

"Yes I did."

"So why did you leave?"

"I wasn't a lifer. I was a good soldier. Maybe even a great soldier. But I served my time. And I got tired of being given orders. I wanted to be my own boss and do what I wanted to do when I wanted to do it. I wanted to see the world without my gun. And I didn't want to think about the possibility of dying so I got out during peace time even though truly for the military there is no peace time just less wars or battles happening."

"And I'm sure your making more money know too?"

"That I am."

"How up are you on your finances? I'm not asking how much money you make just are you aware of your personal financial picture especially when it comes to your business?"

"Nobody counts my money but me so I'm up on them."

"And you're a Republican. So are you a conservative republican at least when it comes to the economy and things like the deficit?"

"I'd say so."

"Then what if I said there is no such thing as the deficit? I'm not sure if he's crazy or a genius but I was listening to some guy talk about it the other day."

"If you're talking about the federal deficit I'd say you're crazy. You and that guy. And if you really believe that it would taint everything you said so far today."

"You have to listen to others before you decide if you agree with them or not. So let me clarify and expound upon my statement. What if I said the way the economy is set up, including the deficit, the way it is run it is designed is to keep poor people poor."

"I'd agree but I'd disagree. Yes the system is set up to keep people poor especially with welfare. But every person has a chance to pull themselves out of that poverty. They just have to take it."

"See we agree on some things. But let's see how far down the rabbit hole you'll go with me. I agree with you about welfare. Anytime you give someone a handout, a constant handout you incentivize them to keep their hand out."

"I agree. But I never thought I would hear a black person say that."

"Do you know how many black people, hardworking, get up every morning and go their jobs, maybe jobs they hate, hate people on welfare. Not necessarily hate the people but hate the system. Most black people believe people on welfare who are able to work should work."

"Welfare, it should not be given to anyone for their entire life."

"I agree, you're right. It was designed to be a hand up, a starting point to help you get back on your feet when needed not some lifelong lifeline. But this is why I say the system is rigged against the poor. It's the same reason why there are so many people in the middle class."

"You just lost me."

"Most people on welfare are scared to get off welfare because they don't know how they are going to eat without it. It's like the old parable, if you give a man a fish he'll eat for that day. If you teach a man to fish he'll eat forever. That's what welfare is. They're giving out fishes and not teaching people to fish. They portion out what they are going to give you and people get comfortable with the little they are given. Now if you make a certain amount you don't qualify so to not lose the benefits people don't work. They'll do whatever which is actually nothing to stay under whatever the line is."

"Ok but what does that have to do with the middle class. The middle class are hardworking people."

"They are. Most middle class people, especially ones with families and kids, most middle class adults are not employed in the field they want and in a lot of cases went to school for. They are not doing what they want to be doing in life. But whatever they are doing pays the bills. It feeds their families. Going out on a limb to chase their dreams is scary. What happens if I fail. It's hard to put one's family at risk to chase a dream. So most middle class families never leave middle class because they get content with what they have. They want more but they are scared of losing what they have, which I understand."

"That's why I didn't have a family until later in life. I couldn't put other people through what I was going through when I was building my business."

"It's why most entrepreneurs, builders of new business start right out of college."

"Or drop out of college."

"Or drop out of college. It's easy to put it on the line when it's just you but when you have mouths to feed they need to be feed so maybe you settle."

"But what does that have to do with the deficit?"

"The federal deficit is an arbitrary number. It's a measurement of how much money we owe ourselves as a country. It's not a measure of how the economy is doing presently. They have other indicators for that. If you owe me a hundred dollars, but I don't care about the hundred and you never repay me does it really matter."

"I always pay my debts."

"Me too but I'm talking figuratively. Let me say it like this. How much money have you spent on your kids. Think about it. Right now our children if you add up the cost we've spent on them thus far, those kids they are working at a deficit to us, their parents."

"Money we're never going to ask for back."

"Right. A deficit that will go unpaid. What's really important is our ability to feed, clothe, and educate them."

"Ok."

"Money on a governmental level of finance is shell game. We as a people pay into it but we are always working at a deficit. But bills always get paid. And when the government wants to build or purchase something they do. Every conservative money hawk watching the deficit in a governmental role will for the right cause raise the deficit. Because it's just a number on a piece of paper. Like what your kids would owe you if you add it up."

"That make a little sense but the government is itself a businesses. Any business can not for long keep operating with a deficit. The business would shut down."

"Unless that business is continuing to grow. If one can see that future profits will eventually exceed the losses people like venture capitalists will pour money into it. But the government is not a business. The government is the rule maker. And they can make any rules they want. It's the reason the country is no longer on the gold standard. Because we have way more money than its equivalent in gold. We have gold, we have crops, we have this and that which all add to our economy."

"Then what rule would you want if not balancing the deficit?"

"I'm not saying this deficit thing is true but it is interesting. And to answer your question regardless of the deficit I believe the government should offer free college. The only way to take people out of poverty is to educate them."

"What's the but? I see a but coming."

"But access has to be equal. It can't be run like our school system is being run now where suburban schools are treated better than inner city schools. The government should have no role in college education other than paying the bills. You should still have to get accepted into college or a trade school or whatever just let Uncle Sam pay the bill. If New York state can do it the federal government can do it."

"Education is definitely the key. After I left the military I went to business school. I knew what I wanted to do but I didn't know how to do it."

"At least not without getting ripped off?"

"Right. But how do you keep the playing field equal for all. Because isn't affirmative action just the opposite of that. If you're going to talk about free college shouldn't the acceptance to those colleges be equal. Isn't affirmative action a form of welfare, a handout? How do you stop schools from using race as a prerequisite to college especially if I'm, we're paying for it?"

"Affirmative action was created to give black people a chance. You're a white man from the south and a business owner. If you're hiring an executive for your business you're going to hire the person you feel most comfortable with. All things being equal you'd hire a white man from the south. Why? Because he's like you. What affirmative action was intended to do was to force employers to give people with the resume for the job a chance, an opportunity. People who are deserving of the opportunity and the job. But let's be honest here. I don't know of one person who has gotten a job because of affirmative action. Have you ever employed someone because of it?"

"No. But it still comes into place for a lot of schools, colleges and their acceptances."

"And once schooling is equal I'd say get rid of it. Colleges can't be filled with rich prep students who never had to worry about what they were going to eat, when all they had to do was study. It's a lot easier to study when you can afford tutors in your home library then when your stomach is grumbling. That's not the kid's fault."

"I understand, and I'm not even saying I disagree but is it fair to the kid who didn't get into the school of their choice because the school wanted a diverse population. How is that equal?"

"It may not be equal. But it is fair. Isn't it fair to look into a student's background. Just like a business who even when working at a deficit can get loans and venture capitalists to buy in because they can see what the company can be in the future, to take that chance."

"But these aren't corporations, these are people, people who worked hard for what they want. Don't they deserve it more than another kid who didn't meet the same grades?"

"If all things were equal yes. If they grew up in the same neighborhood, went to the same school, then yes. But you know like I know things are never equal. I'll take a chance on the kid who rose from the concrete to better his or her life every time. I'll take the kid who worked hard for the A through difficult circumstances over the kid who never had to struggle and was given everything."

"And that kid would deserve it but at the detriment of someone who did better academically?"

"Everything can't be about straight academics. You have to look at other factors. What that kid who did great academically needs to worry about or the kids in their own school. Beat them out for the spot you want. Compare yourself to those around you not those you know nothing about."

"All I can say is Thank God for the internet and phones with cameras."

"Why do you say that?"

"Because now no matter who you are or where you are at the touch of a finger you can see all those things that happen that people never believed happen. Things that can't be covered up. Those cops you think don't do anything wrong. They're being recorded. Nanny cams catching babysitters doing horrible things to babies. Cameras catching cars from hit and runs. Things like that."

"It has also brought us all closer together."

"It has which can be a good or a bad thing."

"There's good and bad in everything. Like those videos you refer to. Most of these videos never show the whole story just a capsule in time most of the time after the fact. You're demanding excellence from, like you say cops are people to. And they have to make split second decisions. And these videos they never show the whole story."

"Some do some don't. But they've been trained. If you can't do the job get out of it. Being a cop is not the job for the faint of heart or the timid. Or the trigger happy. But even if the video doesn't show the whole altercation if it shows the cop did something wrong they did something wrong."

"And except for New York almost every one of those cops were fired and tried in a court of law."

"In a court of law that first takes the word of a cop over any defendant. And almost every one of those cops beat the case even though there was video evidence."

"Then they were innocent."

"They were found innocent that doesn't mean they were."

"In the eyes of the court it does."

"Was OJ guilty?" Pause. "My point exactly. Do you know how cops beat cases?"

"No but I'm sure you're going to tell me."

"Sure am. One cops, their union, prosecutors and judges are all in bed with each other. They have to be. Cops build cases and arrest criminals. Prosecutors use the case the cops built and bring them to trial before the judge. The judge oversees the process in their courtroom."

"And what's wrong there?"

"I'm getting to it. You see the symbiotic relationship they all have. They all need each other. If one of the three is missing criminals stay on the street."

"Get to your point."

"My point is when cops come to trial they almost always ask for a bench trial. No jury, no public in the process. Just the cop, the FOP and their lawyers who almost always back the cop, then the prosecutor and the judge. A prosecutor who doesn't want to piss off the FOP too much because they'll need their help to continue doing their job in the next case. You can't prosecute people and lock them up if the cops aren't arresting people. If the cops aren't investigating. Can't keep the bad guys off the street that way. And in almost all cases the judge finds them innocent. A little convenient don't you think."

"Cops take bench trials because the public can be unfair especially when there is a video, a video without context. Judges can see through that. There's no conspiracy there just a cop trying to get a fair trial. And you're insinuating these prosecutor aren't doing their best job. That's wrong. Those prosecutors do everything in their power to get convictions for those cops. They would never undermine their own prosecution. Stats matter in that profession. And why all this focus on the bad cops. Don't you think besides the fact that we now have video proof that the fact cameras are everywhere it stops a lot of bad things from happening?"

"Of course it does. Those people who want to blame the cops for something they didn't do. Oh yeah what are you going to falsely accuse them of now. It goes both ways now. Nah that cop didn't hit you and you know he didn't. Police body cameras have cut down on false accusations by the public in large numbers. Those videos also show how tolerant and how much these cops put up with. There's plenty of videos where if the cop hit the person, the cop would have been wrong cops can't go around hitting people but I would have understood. I know we kill cops but like I said the overwhelming majority of cops are good people they're just being stereotyped right now by the public because of the few bad cops. Don't you think if police forces across the nation would do things to get rid of the bad cops things would change? And if we actually started convicting cops when they cross the line?"

"This justice system of ours isn't perfect but it's better than anywhere else."

"Just because it's the best doesn't mean it can't be better. Now these cameras, cameras make everybody think before they act because everybody now has a camera in their hand. It also makes everyone tell the truth. Well almost everyone."

"You really have this thing against the police don't you."

"I do not. I love the police. I have friends who are cops. And not associates I'm talking good friends. Been in my house multiple times. Know my wife and kids, great friends. Both black, white and other. Both male and female. I have love for the police. But just because I have love for them doesn't mean I won't criticize them, call them out when they are wrong. Like I said earlier I love my kids but when they are wrong I let them know. And like I also said before 99.99 percent of cops are good decent people. It's a shame but, like I said before, I hope they understand the way they feel know, the way they feel they are being portrayed unfairly, that's the way a whole community feels they have been treated forever by those same people. Some would say it's karma. Messed up aint it."

"I think you said that before."

"Some things need to be said again."

"So you can criticize the police but you can't or won't criticize your own people."

"And how should we be criticized?"

"Do you know what white people do better than black people?"

"What's that?"

"We act in concert when it comes to our money. What do you think golf clubs and private clubs are for? It's not for golfing and working out only. It's where business gets done. I don't think your community knows the power they have financially. We don't even need to say we're not going to support something, we just do it. Fair or unfair. Look at your schools. Some white man or more than likely group of white men somewhere decided not to fund them equally. Someone who was voted in to office by the way. Why do your neighborhoods fail? Because no one puts out the finances to fix them. You as a group fight so much amongst yourselves you never get out of situations as a whole. Yes, slowly more and more black people are making it out of the 'hood' but it's still one or two at a time. You don't build businesses and give back. You don't build wealth. You make it and leave and become rich. Then rich where white people don't look at you as black anymore. Yeah I know it's a thing because it's not a black vs white thing really. I mean it is but more than anything it's a poor vs rich thing. Then once you make it you don't look at yourself as black anymore either. You disassociate yourself with where you came from like your better than. That's what rich people do. Now you're rich and black and trying to make more money because you think that is the key to life then you have to go to a meeting with white people to get it okayed. Yup, there are a lot of Uncle Tom's out there. Yes I said it. You think Trump is the devil's proxy, but I bet you he can always find a token Unc to put in a picture with him. And this is a white guy saying this. But why? There's enough money in the black community, in your community to fix your own problems but you don't. If black people pulled together and started their own you could be so powerful. But you fight amongst yourselves. You have to be flashy. You have to have the biggest car. Fuck public schools if they aren't working. Build you own. LeBron is but why is he the only one. Oprah built one in Africa. But why are they the only one's not trying to make more money off the struggle. I mean I'm sure there are more that I'm not aware of but not enough. Start your own private schools, give a great education and charge fifty thousand a year. Start your own prep schools. But no. If black people as a community, as a financial entity choose they could shut down most companies, or at least hold them hostage. Without your money they would go broke. But it will never happen. Man I think as a group of people you all have PTSD. You're still harping on slavery. Asking for forty acres and a mule and all that. Why. It's never going to happen. Move past it. Until your mindset looks forward you'll never do it. I want to say everything I just said is just my opinion but it's not its fact."

"But if one doesn't know their history they are doomed to repeat it. Why do you think they killed Dr. King?"

"After all I just said that's your response. What kind of question is that?"

"Humor me. Why do you think they killed Dr. King? Because of precisely what you just said. He was mobilizing the entire black population. And he brought white people with him. They didn't want that. And when I say they I mean those in power. Whoever made the call, whoever greenlit his execution."

"So you're saying Martin Luther King was killed by the government?"

"I'm saying I don't know who authorized his assassination and planned it, it could have been someone in the government or just some group of rich people who thought he was getting to powerful, motivating and mobilizing too many black faces. I don't know who was behind it but what I do know it may have been James Earl Ray that pulled the trigger, maybe, but it wasn't his idea. If he was the shooter it took meticulous planning, planning he wasn't capable of."

"You love your conspiracy theories."

"You were talking about slavery. Slavery subliminally affected white people too. So now I'm really going to talk about conspiracies. We've already talked about the rich versus poor right. We know what slavery did to black people and its lingering effects. But what did slavery do to white people?"

"Huh? Slavery didn't do anything to white people."

"No it did and I learned this from a white person. A white woman from the south like you who moved up north. What slavery did to white people was let them think it was okay to be poor. Because though they never talk about it there are millions of poor white people. There are more poor white people in America then poor black people. What slavery did was it gave poor white people someone to look down on. It told them they weren't at the bottom. It told them it was ok to be poor because at least you're not at the bottom. This is the quote from a poor white person 'I may be poor but at least I'm not a nigger'. What kind of backward thinking is that?"

"I've heard that before where I grew up."

"And there weren't even any black people there. Like we've both said until we as people learn it's not black vs white its rich vs poor we'll be stuck. If the 99% on non-rich people could put their differences aside and move forward as a unit imagine what would get done. But I'm going to go back to the assassinations I was just talking about before I forget. And the cohesiveness of the black community or lack of. Let's not think this country doesn't have a history of assassinating people who are trying to pull up and help the black community. Not only was Dr. King inspiring black people he was mobilizing them. And the scariest part of all he had white people actively involved in the process. That's why he died. That's why he was murdered. So this country's history of killing people, remember the man who spearheaded the 13th Amendment to the Constitution, the amendment that freed the slaves was murdered, assassinated, executed."

"A republican remember."

"Back when the Republican Party wasn't a front for rich white people. But let's start with Lincoln and the 13th amendment."

"Wait the Emancipation Proclamation freed black people first."

"No it didn't. If you read it, it says and I'm paraphrasing here, but it says by proclamation I free all slaves in states held in armed rebellion. Basically meaning Lincoln freed the slaves only of the states of the Confederacy. States who at that time he had no power over. He also waited until the north was losing the war to do it. He freed those slaves so they could fight in the union army and they helped turn the tide. If you look at it, it was a genius chess move because the Union was going to lose the Civil War until this happened."

"So you're saying Lincoln wasn't really interested in freeing the slaves."

"I can't say definitely either way. From what I've read he genuinely thought slavery was wrong but he also had no plans of doing anything about it if you read what he said prior to the civil war. He was no abolitionist. If you think the civil war was about slavery you're wrong. The civil war was about the same things states are fighting about now. Why those people in Texas keep talking about seceding. Southern states didn't want to be dictated to about anything from some federal government. Slavery was just one of the things they didn't want orders from because they saw it coming to an end as most northern states ended the policy. States wanted to dictate their own policy especially southern states who saw things differently than northern states. Sound familiar."

"Let me cut in and tell you about Lincoln's killer. Down south, wait let me not speak for the whole south, at least where I grew up John Wilkes Booth was somewhat of a cult hero. Publicly General Lee is the man, the myth, the idol."

"I never understood that didn't he lose?"

"Crazy part is he said the same thing. He didn't want to be remembered because he lost."

"But Booth, where I grew up, he is the man. Even though the north won the war he fought against the tyrannical oppressors. He killed Lincoln in retaliation for the destruction Lincoln brought. And not only Lincoln, he was trying to kill Lincoln and all those around him. Sent his boys after the other people. They don't talk about that much."

"I've never heard anything like that before."

"It may be only a few who think like that but I've definitely heard it whispered before. This was his revenge for the south."

"Ok then."

"Continue on. Didn't mean to interrupt."

"Whatever the explanation Lincoln was assassinated after freeing the slaves. Mere months after the 13th amendment was passed Lincoln was killed. For revenge for the south or revenge for losing or revenge for freeing the slaves or more likely all of it, it happened."

"It did."

"Now let's get out the 1800's and move forward to 1963. President John Fitzgerald Kennedy was assassinated. No way Oswald acted alone as modern day ballistics will tell you no single bullet could have done the damage it did at the angles it did to multiple people. Whether you believe that or not is up to you. Even if you believe he was the lone perpetrator it doesn't matter to my point. Now follow the trail here. In 1963 JFK was murdered. JFK, a man who believed in equal rights for black people. Less than a year and a half later Malcom X was murdered."

"By his own people."

"By his own people yes. The gunman was one of his own but is thought to have been trained by the FBI to assassinate him."

"Why would the FBI want to kill Malcolm X?"

"I'm glad you asked that? Let me explain. For two reasons. One, at the time Malcom X and Dr. King were the two greatest unifiers of black people and their voices were growing stronger, starting to cross to the other side of the country and the world. This at a time before the internet and cell phones. And from what you hear they were ready to start working together."

"But them working together doesn't explain why Malcolm X was killed by the FBI as you say."

"It is known the FBI was keeping tabs on Malcom X but of course they won't release them. Just like they won't release the full unredacted files on JFK. Do you know anything about Malcolm X?"

"I know more about Dr. King but I know who Malcolm X is. He was Dr. King but Muslim and not against violence."

"There's way more to the story and the man than that but for now we'll go with what you know except I need to add the fact he only used violence as a way of self-defense. Now if this is war and you have two opponents who do you take care of first? The opponent who will match your violence with violence in return and will not turn the other cheek or the opponent who will match your violence with peace and will turn the other cheek? I can see by your face you're starting to follow me now. You kill Malcom X because then the biggest loudest most respected voice left is a preacher man preaching non-violent resistance. Now remember Malcom X was killed a little more than a year after JFK so you have two voices promoting equality assassinated. One wielding the power of the federal government, the other wielding the pent up frustration of black people ready to act. So what you're left with is Dr. King telling you violence is not the answer. This non-violent leader they let live for a couple more years. Dr. King, he calmed the waters when it came to the use of violence as a tactic of defense. Then three short years after Malcom X was killed Dr. King was killed, assassinated, executed. But not until after he spread his approach of non-violence. Then three months later Robert Kennedy was murdered. A man who was trying to push his brother's agenda. Within a five year span four people were murdered, assassinated because they were pro-black equality."

"Don't say executed I got it."

"Four people trying to improve the plight of black people were taken by somebody or somebodies."

"You're nuts. It takes a lot of moving parts to string that crazy theory together."

"People once thought it was crazy to think the world was round. They thought the Wright brother were crazy for trying to fly. So think what you wish. Now back to your statement from before I got into all this. You wonder why we black people can't come together. Because every time we do somebody gets killed. Our leaders get killed."

"What about Obama?"

"I have nothing negative to say about President Obama nor his wife. He ran the office for eight years with class and dignity and showed black people what they can aspire to be. Showed everyone what education can do. But Obama was the President. He did things for the greater good of the country as a President should. He wasn't focused on black people, he couldn't be even though he never left us behind. There's a little difference there."

"Even if what you said was true which it isn't, it's been fifty years since all those things occurred. What you're doing right now is making excuses. As a community since you always refer to all black people like all black people are the same, once your community realizes your own power you could do great things. Until then Oprah will be great, Will Smith will be great, LeBron will be great, the Obamas will be great, individual people will be great but your community won't be."

"You know what the sad part about this is, to a certain degree, hearing you say it and not being biased by the speaker, I agree with you so I'm going to let you live. We as a people, both individually and collectively, we need to do better."

"What do you mean you're going to let me live?"

"Relax it's just an expression. Meaning I'm going to let you have that. I don't have anything to say negative about it."

"'Cause we can go to war now if you want."

Laugh

"Like I said when we walked in, I'm not here to fight. I'm here to listen, learn and educate."

"Cool. My apologies then."

"None needed."

"So I'm going to let you live about your conspiracy theory."

Laugh "Ok. Why?"

"Because I have my own."

"I have to hear this."

"We never landed on the moon."

"You're one of them."

"I am. It was all done in some Hollywood studio. Why hasn't anyone ever been able to get their hands on the original film? You know why. Because if somebody did and they scaled up the video we would all be able to see the wires."

"Why would the US government want to fake a moon landing?"

"PR. Public relations. Spin. To make the American people believe we beat the Russians and were still the greatest nation on the planet."

"Do you really believe that?"

Laughs

"Nah. I'm just messing with you because you just said some outlandish stuff. Even though what you said makes sense in a logical timeline there is no 'them' that could order something like that. It would be impossible."

"This from the guy who believes in the Illuminati?"

"I never actually said I did."

"I read between he lines. Now this is outlandish but what if the flashy things in Men In Black were real and they have changed our memories?"

"You're joking right?"

"Yeah I'm joking. Am I?" Laughs. "Back to what we were just talking about. You know what I believe is the greatest problem in my community. Missing male figures. Now I'm not saying single moms don't do great jobs raising boys because they do. But a woman can't teach a boy the intricacies of being a man. Just like a dad can't teach his daughter the intricacies of being a woman. That's where the war on drugs hurt my community. That's where Clinton hurt my community. You had a whole generation of men missing. So you had boys who grew up without dads or male figures in their lives teaching them, showing them the way, showing them how to be men. Mom can teach them to be great people and I'll give credit to the moms who do it by themselves. I can't take nothing from them but they're not dad. I know people don't want to hear it but it's true."

"After doing some reflection and listening if I'm being honest. You know what I believe the greatest problem in my community is? Fear. The 1% at the top. When you're at the perch looking over you don't want to come off it. And you really want to know why? Because they fucked over so many people on the way up they're afraid they'll get that same treatment on their way up. The rest of us, the non 1%. You call it white privilege. No one wants to admit it but it's real even all the way down to the poorest. No one wants to give that up. White privilege is awesome. Even though they will never admit it we see the way other races are treated. We don't want to be treated like that. No sir. Know how I know?"

"How?"

"Look at the sexual misconduct stuff that's happening in Hollywood, with Weinstein and others. MeToo. Thandi Newton, who I love, I think she is beautiful, a great actress, so underrated. Probably should have said great actress first but years ago she came out and exposed a director and his casting couch. It was crazy stuff, unthinkable and inexcusable stuff. She exposed some of the stuff in Hollywood but no one did anything. No one cared. There was no MeToo movement then. Not for Thandi Newton. You know what. It took a bunch of white women to come out and let their voices be heard before voices were heard."

"I'm glad you can admit that."

"I don't know if I could have before today. Or even once I leave this room and go back out there to the real world."

"I'll never be able to walk in your shoes. Just like I feel bad for the cops who have to deal with the aftermath of the bad cops I feel bad for white people."

"Huh?"

"Not all white people are bad. You never owned a slave. You never, I hope, acted in a purposefully racist way. But because of some in your community you have to answer the question."

"When you look at white people do you ask yourself if they're racist?"

"I don't. I always let actions speak for a man because words lie. But just as I'm not a thief or a drug dealer you're not a racist. Maybe unaware of certain things but that's why we're talking. Every white person shouldn't have to answer for the sins of their fathers."

"Thanks. Can I go back to something we talked about earlier?"

"Sure."

"Alright. Speaking of cameras. Me and a friend of mine got into a heated debate and I want your opinion. It has to do with a lot of the stuff we've been talking about all day plus it involves women. So what do you think of the football player incident, the one where while the guy was still a college player, he punched the girl in the face?"

"My honest opinion. He was dead wrong for hitting that girl. Never should have done it. I think he paid a fine and did some community service. He got off easy. That being said she should have never put her hands on him. He's an asshole for reacting to some girl slapping him."

"And the racist taunts from her boyfriend, friend, whoever dude was. An accusation he denies but I don't believe him. But whatever. And she spit on him."

"I don't believe him either. Kids say and do stupid stuff and more often than not they believe what they say but change their tune when they get caught. And he was drinking. You know they say alcohol is the real truth elixir."

"Yeah, we call it liquid courage."

"Look at the New Jersey girl who got kicked out of Alabama and congrats to the school because she should have been."

"Never heard about that one. What happened?"

"She made a really racist video saying she hates black people but using the n-word. Then when she was called out on it she made another video saying she can say whatever she wants n-word n-word n-word just kept saying it. Said she's in school in the south so she can say whatever she wants. Oh yeah it was on Martin Luther King Day and she said I don't care that it's Martin Luther King Day. Alabama kicked her out of school then she wanted to apologize."

"Wow."

"But back to the football player. Even though we both believe the girl's friend said something racial to him he should not have followed her back inside that store. Sometimes you have to let ignorance go and walk away. I know it's hard but in life you have to make hard decisions and he made a terrible one. If there were racist taunts he has to learn to let it go. Be the bigger man. I know sometimes that's hard especially for young men of all races but it's a learned trait, something that will lead all kids to better things as they grow. You don't have to fight all fights."

"Literally, especially against a girl."

"Especially against a girl. But on the other hand if she doesn't spit in his face and slap him she doesn't get her jaw broke. That's the fact. She could have walked away too. I'm not saying his reaction was wrong but it was a reaction. I think it's why he got off so light with the police."

"You don't think it had anything to do with his stature as a football player."

"I don't think so. I think they saw he was hit first. Women always want equal rights and they should have them and that includes not putting your hands on anyone. I think if she was a man nothing would have happened to the football player and probably the person who hit him would have been arrested."

"So do you think this was a case of white privilege?"

"No. I think this was a case of stupid drunk girl not thinking there were consequences to her actions. I think all women in general. And let me be very careful how I say these words. But when women, some women I'll say, when some women are arguing with you, once they get mad they take what they say and what they do to some other level. They will say the most vile, heinous stuff to get a reaction out of you. Most guys don't want to argue. Some women, they'll throw stuff at you hit you knowing you're not going to hit them back. That's not what men do. We just want to fix the situation and move on. That angers them even more. And yes I'm generalizing, not all women are like this but some are. And a hurt mad woman will say all kinds of stuff, they'll start talking bad about your mama, about the way you are in bed, all kinds of stuff whose only purpose is to hurt. They don't care if it is not true because they're mad. They know they can't hurt you physically so they try to hurt you mentally."

"You know when you're mad you speak the truth more often than not. The bottled up truth but go on."

"But when women say those things they say it knowing the man standing in front of them. They know most men aren't going to hit them. Most men are just going to take it. They may punch a wall or knock something over in frustration but most men won't hit a woman no matter how far she takes it."

"You're right there. Shoot I had a woman call me all kinds of pussy once and then say to me 'what, you going to hit me now.' I just had to walk away."

"Exactly. I think that's where that girl was. I think she thought she could say and do whatever and there would be no consequences. Then with one reaction, one thoughtless reaction it all changed. But I'm not excusing him. Not at all, it was a cowardly move. He was a punk for doing it but she did hit him first."

"But he broke her jaw."

"He did. Laid her out. That was crazy. He's lucky he got off the way he did. Again he was dead wrong, no excuse, be a man and walk away. But again if she didn't hit and spit on him there's no reaction. Spitting on someone is almost the most foul thing you can do."

"So would you have drafted him? Because I would have for all the reasons you just said. And he had no other incidents on his record."

"He could be a good kid but I wouldn't have drafted him. Like we've talked about cops having to accept responsibility, even for one act I think he should have."

"But he paid his debt. Doesn't he deserve a second chance?"

"He did and he does. I just don't know if I would have given it to him. I also wouldn't knock someone for giving it to him. It's a difficult question. I don't know if I would think the same if I didn't have a daughter."

"I just think he didn't start the incident. I can't hold up his future for something he didn't instigate. His reaction was abhorrent but I kind of understand."

"I'm not agreeing or disagreeing with you but let me ask you this. In general we hold these athletes to a high standard."

"We do but they're getting paid a lot. As an employer you want to make sure you're getting a return on your investment. And fans pay the bills so you can't have them turn on you and stop spending money."

"But isn't it a standard we don't hold anyone else to in real life. We don't hold our coworkers to it. Is that fair? How many of your coworkers have DUI's or in your case your employees. You don't know. But we know as soon as it happens to every athlete and then the public wants to castrate them. How many of our coworkers or employees have criminal records, or better yet just accusations of battery, domestic violence, or orders of protection out against them? We don't know and we don't care but we want these athletes to be something other than a regular human being."

"They're paid millions. They're stadiums are built with public money. They should be held accountable."

"So it's all about how much their paid?"

"No. It's because their public figures. Public figures should be held to a higher standard."

"All public figures?"

"All public figures!"

"Except the President of the United States?"

Pause. "How do you always bring everything back to him?"

"Just asking?"

"Yes him to. But you're stuck with him until his term is up. Then if after four years he hasn't done a good enough job the country can vote him out. Until then he is The President."

"Ok back to the girl who the football player hit. Is it her responsibility not to get hit?"

"What do you mean?"

"Is it the responsibility of the girl not to get hit?"

"It's her responsibility in life not to put herself in bad situations. What if when she hit that table she broke her neck and was paralyzed or died. Yes he shouldn't have hit her we all get that. But if she never instigated the situation she never gets hit. There's no way you can argue that. Now if she was my daughter I would have tried to kill that kid because he was dead wrong. I have a daughter. And I want her to understand you want to come home every night. Never put yourself in a bad situation. Never place yourself in harm's way unless you're a cop or fire fighter or soldier, then it's your job but other than that I hope she knows to walk away. Do you need to prove your point or do you want to be alive? I don't ever want to have to hate some man for doing something to my daughter. Yeah, he better not do it. But I would want my baby to walk away. I know it's not her fault but I don't want anything to ever happen to her. Just like if her and her girlfriends go out. No they shouldn't have to worry about somebody ruffying their drinks but it happens and if they put their drinks down they need to say down. We all wish it was a utopia but this earth isn't and we have to live in what we have."

"In that girls' case she got paid though."

"If I was on that trial she wouldn't have gotten a penny. Now don't get me wrong he deserved to go to jail. He deserved a harsher penalty than he got so if I was him every day I'd thank the Lord. But think about this. She's not Monica Lewinsky, Nancy Kerrigan, Anita Hill, see I do know more black people than you think. Even though she was attacked she was the instigator, we don't even remember the girl's name and she got her face broken because she has some culpability here. I wouldn't have given here a dime."

"I think they settled out of court."

"Smart move by him. It probably looked good to the NFL. He accepted responsibility but that's just my opinion. She is no angel here."

"But neither is he. Neither was right in this situation."

"Sometimes that is the case."

"You said you are a Christian right?"

"Yes I am."

"Then as a Christian man"

"Wait before you ask whatever you're going to ask know I don't look at myself that way. I'm not a Christian man. I'm a man who believes in the Bible, God and Jesus. I'm not a believer in the church or rather its leadership."

"Wait, what? I forgot what I was going to ask. What does what you just said even mean?"

"The church, whatever denomination is a fraud. Now again I'm going to say I am a Christian. I believe in the tenets of the Bible. But historically and its really ridiculous right now, historically the church has not worked for its people only for itself."

"Explain."

"During Jesus' time he fought with the Pharisees and Sadducees. If anyone amongst you is without sin throw the first stone. Then there were the Crusades. During the Crusades the church didn't preach and tell people how they should live they tried to force people, at the pointy end of a sword, to live a certain way. We talk about Muslins and 9/11 but how many abortion clinics were blown up in the name of God? How many people were enslaved in the name of God? How many pedophiles did and probably still are, how many is the Catholic Church hiding?"

"What brought you around to this way of thinking?"

"I think it was like 2010, 2011 somewhere around there. CNN did a survey of evangelical leaders and more than half said tithing isn't mandatory. Then I went and asked my pastor and I was told tithing is an Old Testament thing. It is not mandatory and the CNN survey was accurate but tithing is something the church relies on to function. So even though it is not mandatory it is how the church operates. It felt like a burden was lifted from me but I thought I was lied to for years. They said you have to do this they didn't say we need you to do this for the benefit of."

"You felt some kind of way."

"I did. I felt betrayed. So what else are they not telling us you know? Then I kept hearing about this prosperity gospel preaching that's going on."

"And you feel like they are crooks?"

"I do. I've read the Bible from back to front. If you read it there's only one promise in the entire Bible. That if you believe God, that Jesus was His Son and you confess your sins to God you'll get to Heaven. That's it. There's nothing in there that promises you anything else."

"This prosperity gospel thing really bothers you."

"It does. They're robbing people, telling them what they want to hear. Telling them that if they give they will get rich. That God wants everybody to be rich. That's not what the Bible says. You can't buy your way to Heaven and you can't buy your way to blessings here on Earth. Both the rain and the sun shine down on both those who believe and those who don't believe. Even those who don't believe are still children of the Lord. My kids, if one of them went away and did something I didn't agree with I'd still love them, they're still my kids. These prosperity preachers they're modern day swindlers peddling fake healing potions. If someone tells you to buy a prayer cloth they're a crook. They're flying around in jets and driving hundred thousand dollar cars because their flock is giving and they aren't even doing the minimum, giving the truth back."

"Ok. Now I remember what I was going to ask you before you got me all off track. What I wanted to ask was since you're a Christian man what do you feel about gay people?"

"What do you mean what do I feel about gay people, they're people. I'm not sure what you're trying to ask me."

"What I'm trying to ask is if you're a Christian, how do you reconcile what the Bible says about everyday life and your interactions with gay people in everyday life? Basically, do you feel being gay is a sin?"

"That's a very loaded question."

"The Bible does say homosexuality is wrong."

"This is the way I look at it. Whether homosexuality is right or wrong is not for me to say. To be truthful it's not something I understand. Me personally I don't know how a man can look at another man and be attracted. But I had a conversation with this young lady once. She was a straight woman and we were talking about another person we both knew. A man who lives as a woman. And I said the same thing to her I just said to you. It's something I don't understand. And I'll never forget what she told me. She said then it's not for you to understand. You don't live that person's life you live your own, worry about you and your family. My outlook changed after that. I'm not here to judge, it's not what I was put on this earth to do. But even if you believe it to be wrong we all have sinned and come short of the glory of God and there is no sin greater than another. So even if it is wrong so is cheating on your wife or husband. That's sexual immorality. And pre-marital sex and masturbation and lust so no strip-clubs even if you're not touching. No thinking about it, that's wrong too. So to be truthful where I'm at in my life I could care less. I don't care who you're sleeping with as long as you're both consenting adults, as long as you're not out here trying to pick up kids, or drugging people or rapping women or grooming boys then sleeping with them and then being hidden by the Catholic Church for centuries. I don't care about if he or she is gay. I don't. Are they good people? Are they good neighbors? Are they law-abiding citizens? That's what I care about."

"Did you always think that way?"

"No. But I also never knew, well growing up I never knew anyone who was open about being gay. Maybe if I did I would have thought differently earlier. I was always told it was wrong so you believe what you were told especially since it was being told to you by adults."

"Then?"

"Then I grew up. I met some gay people. At one point in life I thought gay people shouldn't get married because that what I was taught. I thought gay people shouldn't be able to raise kids because that's what I was taught. Then you meet gay people, good upstanding citizens and you learn that's all a bunch of nonsense. In this country there is a separation of church and state for a reason. Even if you disagree with their life how is their life hurting you? And why are you so worried about their sins and not your own? If you believe homosexuality to be a sin, why are we so pressed on this one sin and not all the myriad of others people commit every day?"

"But the reason that we have men and women is to have babies and populate the earth? Gay couples can't do that."

"But what they can do is take on the children that straight people had and left to the wayside. How many kids are out there waiting for adoption? How many straight couples are horrible people, terrible parents? And you don't want to let them raise kids because they are gay. Thirteen kids that California couple starved. They weren't gay. They're regular people they're just attracted to who they're attracted to."

"It doesn't make you queasy?"

"Queasy? No. Do I still have a long way to go in being totally comfortable? Yes. Look I'm a man and whether we want to admit it or not men and women don't even look at gay people the same. Most heterosexual men don't have a problem with gay women. Why? Because deep down at one point or another we want to be in a threesome with them. It's a fantasy all heterosexual men have had. Plus we don't feel threatened by gay women. Maybe a little by the butch ones but that's because they're taking women we want. Women who don't want us by the way. And even then, if she's gay but cute we're like she still has a fat ass or she still has some big tits. We would still have sex with her if she let us even though she doesn't want us, not at all. Then there's gay men. And here's where the double standard comes in. We separate gay men into two categories. Regular gay men who act like regular heterosexual men. Am I saying anything that isn't true?"

"No, you're good keep going."

"Then there's the flamboyant gay men. If we're being honest those are the ones I'm not truly comfortable around. But that's not on them that's on me. Look be who you are. I don't care but I'm not all the way there yet."

"Is it the pocketbooks and the dressing like women? The J. Edgar Hoover's?"

"It's the way I was raised and truthfully the way I raised my son. You are a boy who will become a man. You are not a girl. It's the effeminate nature of not being a man that still, I'm still not comfortable with. Men don't suck their teeth. Put some bass in your voice those kind of things. But like I said that's me. I'm not fully there yet."

"So you believe in gender roles in society?"

"Actually no I don't but yes so yes and no. I believe anything a man can do a woman can do. You want to fight in the military go ahead. You want to be President go ahead. You want to be CEO go ahead. You want to be a cop or firefighter go ahead. You want to play football go ahead. But at the end of the day I still want a man to still be a man. Not a sexist pig or a rapist or anything like that but a man holds the door for a lady. A man walks on the outside near the street. A man pulls out a chair. Men don't wear dresses and pocketbooks. Men are not women. So when I see that kind of gay man I still shake my head. I know I shouldn't and I'm getting better but"

"But"

"I shouldn't be that way. I don't judge but that still irks me. And it's not because the Bible says it's wrong it's just me."

"So what are you saying really?"

"What I'm saying is I think any person can fulfill any role, can be whatever they aspire to be professionally and personally. But I also think there are differences between women and men. I want my daughter to be a woman. If she wants to play basketball go play. When she's playing I want her in ball shorts and sneaks giving it to whoever thinks she's not good enough. Then when the game is over be able to put on a dress or sweatpants and be cute, be a little girl, a young lady. For my son I want the same thing sort of. When he's playing basketball he should take no prisoners. But after the game be a boy. I don't know if I can really explain it. No I don't want my son wearing dresses. Dresses are for girls. No my son is not a princess he is a prince. No he shouldn't have a tiara. Now I'm not saying my daughter couldn't rule. She could be queen and be the baddest ruler ever. Understand what I'm trying to say?"

"I get you. But what if one of your children turned out to be gay? Then how would you feel?"

"Listen I don't want either of my kids to be gay especially my son. Why, because I'm a heterosexual male and that is what I want from my son and his sister to be quite honest. But if they are gay. Yeah it would hurt me in the beginning but I'm not going to stop loving them. I'm not kicking them out my life. They have a life and a choice to make. I can't live their life for them. I'm going to love them regardless."

"So you believe homosexuality is a choice?"

"I don't know and I don't care. I don't think it really matters. I don't spend any time thinking about it or trying to figure it out."

"It does matter because if it's biological it can't be changed. If it's a choice it can be."

"Again it doesn't matter to me. Each person has their life to live and what you do in the privacy of your home has nothing to do with me. You should be allowed to live your life the way you want as long as it doesn't interfere with another person living theirs. When it comes to religion each person has their own life to live and choice to make. Whether you like it or not it's why we have free will. It's why we are not robots. If you believe homosexuality to be wrong then you believe they will have to face God when they die as everyone will. So let God judge them not me. If that's what someone believes then they have to have a relationship with God. Again that's their relationship with Him not mines. But at the end of the day what you believe should have no bearing. Why? Because they are still people."

"I just don't agree with that."

"You don't have to. But if you keep pressing this issue then why not scream about all the issues of immorality in the Bible. I'm assuming you lost your virginity way before you were married like 99% of all Americans. And you didn't and I'm pretty sure still don't see nothing wrong with it.

Ever watch porn before. Ever beat your, masturbate. Playboy? Are you going to harp on your kids about those things the same way you are about homosexuality? Every day you have a choice to step left or right. Which way you step is none of my business unless you step onto my property. So who cares? Let them be great. And let me say let them not be discriminated against. They are people. They deserve their human rights also. So yes bake them a cake. Discrimination in any form is wrong. That's some nonsense. They're not asking you to sleep with them. They're not even asking you to be okay with what they are doing. Refusing service is not oaky if you're a business. That's a deep dark passage to go down because you know what's next. Other groups start to get discriminated against."

"I may not agree with you about the whole homosexuality aspect being ok. But I do agree we can't discriminate against them. That's ridiculous. Something I don't know I would have said years ago."

"You grow and you learn."

"You grow and you learn. But what if I don't want my child brought up with that. Isn't that my right?"

"First let's not call it that. It's not a disease. You can't catch it. Second it's almost the year 2020. You can't hide from people. You can't shield your children from people. They are going to and have already come into contact with people who are gay and unlike when you and I were young, openly gay. I bet you your children have less problems with it than either you or I have. And I could name hundreds of things I don't want my kids growing up around that I have no choice about including racism. It's called life. Deal with it."

"Though I have an issue with homosexuals, I have less of an issue with grown men and women. What I really have an issue with is kids. Kids being brought up around it like its ok. Like its normal. It's not. No matter what you say to me, no matter what they say to me it's not natural. And maybe I'm just stuck in my ways but kids shouldn't have to be forced to deal with this issue. Adults shouldn't be promoting gayness onto kids."

"Is your son gay?"

"No."

"Then what are you concerned about?"

"I don't want him thinking its ok to 'try' it. It's nothing but the devil and an evil spirit."

"If homosexuality was an evil spirit then it is one that could have been cast out. You need to stop listening to these preachers spewing nonsense teachings from their pulpits. They're going to hell."

"They're just trying to protect us."

"Can you show me in the Bible where it says homosexuality is an evil spirit. No you can't. Just because somebody gets in front of you and says something from a pulpit doesn't mean it's true. You need to read the Bible for yourself so when they say stupid stuff you'll know better. And don't let them take verses out of context, they're good for that too to prove a point."

"I just don't understand how a man can look at another man and think I want to have sex with him. I just can't. It's not what the human male body was made for."

"This goes to my point earlier. You don't really have a problem with homosexuality. You have a problem with gay men. Why? Because you can understand how a woman can look at another woman and thinks she's sexy. It's because we're men. Because we think women are sexy beings. We can relate. And I'll remind you what somebody told me which made me rethink some things. It's not your life. You're not a gay man.

It's not for you to understand. Everybody doesn't understand everything. Don't look at them as gay look at them as people. And if we're going to quote the Bible it says to love thy neighbor as thy would love thyself. But they don't push that aspect of the Bible. Love them. If you think it's wrong pray for them and get out of their way."

"You really have a problem with the church don't you."

"No. The church is the people. It's you, me and everyone else. I love the church. I have a problem with people exploiting the church for financial gain. These 'pastors' are sticking up their people and using the Bible as a gun. That's what I have a problem with. When you won't do anything, even something as simple as saying a prayer without me paying you. It's just so wrong."

"Understood."

"It's why Christians are looked at the way they are sometimes."

"Another example of the mass being judged by the few?"

"Now you're learning."

"It's also why we are under attack."

"We aren't under attack. Not the way people think. As a Christian how can you defend Trump who breaks a commandment every time he speaks? Thou shall not lie. His circle is elitist and racist but again you can ignore that, look past it because it doesn't affect you. How does the Pope who I think they're going to kill"

"Wait what?"

"The Pope. They're going to kill the Pope. His own people. And they may do it in a way we don't even see. He's going to get sick or die in an accident or something like that."

"Why do you think that?"

"Because he's too radical. He's called out his own people for being corrupt. He fights for the poor. When was the last time the Catholic Church publicly fought for the poor? He's going to die at the hands of some modern day Judas, watch."

"You say it so matter of factly."

"The Catholic Church is the most powerful known organization on the face of the planet. And he's messing up the system. He's fucking with people's money. At any level when you mess with people's money bad things happen. Money is the root of all evil even in the church. Watch. They're going to kill him. Just look. The last Pope quit. He'd rather quit than deal with whatever's going on over there. The last Pope to not die Pope was like six hundred years ago. This new Pope, they don't like this guy."

"But the people do."

"The people liked JFK too. And Dr. King. You keep fucking with rich powerful people and their money and their plans. People so entrenched in the system and start messing up their program. Things happen. I'm just saying. I hope it doesn't happen. I'm not Catholic but I like this guy but watch. You'll see. Either they are going to kill him or he is going to miraculously tone down his message. One or the other. And that's what I mean by the war is not what they portray. The war is greed and people using the name of the church for personal gain. And the fact you can't force people to believe. It only pushes them away."

"So you're calling the Catholic church evil?"

"No. I'm calling all churches and church organizations, look once money gets involved things change. These organizations, they don't look out for their flock like they should in my opinion. They look out for themselves. How are pedophile priests still being protected? How are pastors' millionaires? Shouldn't that money be given back to the church and the community they serve? Since we're on the church let me ask you about Christmas."

"What about it?"

"Is Christmas a religious holiday or a secular holiday?"

"It's a religious holiday?"

"Ok. Then when your children were small did you let them believe in Santa Claus?"

"Of course I did. What's the harm?"

"So you're ok with lying to your children. Wait let me finish. You're ok with lying to your children about a holiday that is supposed to celebrate the birth of Jesus Christ and you let it be led by some made up fat man in a suit?"

"It's not a lie."

"It is a lie. There is no such thing as Santa Claus. It's a story we tell little kids. It's a story that has no bearing on the meaning of the holiday."

"Okay it's a lie. But it's a tradition. It's part of the season. It's what makes not just Christmas but the whole season."

"So as a Christian, you have a problem with homosexuality but not one with Santa Claus which means you probably don't have a problem with the Eater Bunny or the Tooth Fairy. All made up lies. Lies that have nothing to do with the reason for celebrating. See the double standard here. It's ok for you but not for them."

"Man it is what it is. Like you said that's life."

"You're not even going to deny it?"

"No. That's the way I fell. I can't fight every fight."

"But don't you see how those, and there are others, don't you see how those double standards come back and haunt Christians. We say love thy neighbor but we don't. Not all of them. Not if their immigrants. But it was ok for this land to be stolen. It's ok for politicians to tout their anti-homosexual policy while having homosexual relations."

"If you have such a problem why don't you join another religion?"

"Because one's faith is not a group thing. It's a personal decision and relationship. You have nothing to do with my faith and I have nothing to do with yours. And because it's what I believe. So I don't put my faith in the leadership nor the leaders because they are people and they have faults and they will let you down so I look to no man or woman for religious leadership, I look to the Book. And unlike most Christians, and I'm not suggesting you do what I did but I have looked at, even though I wasn't interested in joining, I looked at other religions. I wanted to see what they were about how they ticked."

"And?"

"And we, not we because I don't but some of us have a problem have this problem with Muslims. But I like some aspects of what they do. How they move."

"Such as bombing buildings and jihad?"

"How about blowing up abortion clinics and shooting up black churches." Silence. "Then I'll continue on. Muslims don't mess with their holidays. Christmas, a day about Jesus' birth we celebrate with Santa, share it with the secular world. Try that with Ramadan. Try and start calling Ramadan a diet and disrespect their fast."

"So?"

"My point is the Christian church is a microcosm of the bigger world. We can look past certain things but we get hung up on other things. Money and power have become more important than the actual message. And the message from the top down is the wrong message. How can you be a Christian and be a racist? What is God only for white people? God's whose Son's body was brass colored and had hair like wool. How can you be a Christian and look the other way every time a church leader sexually assaults a child and they look the other way? How can you be a Christian or rather, you know what let me say it like this, when Jesus comes back there are going to be a lot of Christians left behind."

"You've given me some things to think about."

"And so have you."

"I know you have to go, meet your wife but we should do this again. But next time we're going to need to bring some women with us. I'm interested in what they would have had to say to all this."

"Definitely. The more diverse the people in the conversation the better the conversation. Would you like to join us, we're just going to grab something to eat? I'd like to introduce you to her."

"My wife's waiting for me too."

"Bring her too."

"Sure. I think she'd like that. Wait until we tell them about this conversation."

Thank you for taking the time to read An Uncomfortable Conversation. Hopefully you'll take this back and talk to your family and friends about what you read. This book is intended to be the start of opening up the conversation and is not the final word. Please remember there is not one person you will agree with 100% of the time on 100% of topics but the conversation can be respectful.

Again Thank You
Derrick Anthony Marrow

Contact Information:

http://www.DerrickMarrow.com
http://www.Facebook.com/DAnthonyM
http://www.Instagram.com/AuthorDerrickMarrow
http://www.Twitter.com/D_Anthony_M

Made in the USA
Middletown, DE
06 June 2020